"I'M NOT 'SUPPOSED TO BE' ANYBODY. I *AM* CAPTAIN NOBODY."

I was all ready to strip off the red sweatpants and put on jeans, but then I stopped. Just wearing the Captain Nobody pants reminded me of the way I'd felt the night before—strong and assured. Confident that Chris was okay. Certain that Mom wouldn't cry anymore. Could I feel that way again?

I slipped on the Captain Nobody shirt with its attached cape, and slid into the silver sneakers.

There! That felt better.

I straightened up and looked at myself in the closet-door mirror.

"What are you doing?" I blurted out to my reflection. "You're still just a scrawny kid."

But then—just for the heck of it—I tugged the mask down over my eyes.

And, what d'you know? All those worries disappeared.

OTHER BOOKS YOU MAY ENJOY

Antsy Does Time	Neal Shusterman
The Big One-oh	Dean Pitchford
Hank the Cowdog #1: The Original Adventures of Hank the Cowdog	John R. Erickson
Hank the Cowdog #2: The Further Adventures of Hank the Cowdog	John R. Erickson
Raymond and Graham: Dancing Dudes	Mike Knudson
Raymond and Graham Rule the School	Mike Knudson & Steve Wilkinson
The Schwa Was Here	Neal Shusterman
The Time Warp Trio #1: The Knights of the Kitchen Table	Jon Scieszka
The Time Warp Trio #2: The Not-So-Jolly Roger	Jon Scieszka
Vet Volunteers #1: Fight for Life	Laurie Halse Anderson
Vet Volunteers #2: Homeless	Laurie Halse Anderson

CAPTAIN NOBODY

DEAN PITCHFORD

PUFFIN BOOKS
An Imprint of Penguin Group (USA) Inc.

PUFFIN BOOKS
Published by the Penguin Group
Penguin Young Readers Group, 345 Hudson Street, New York, New York 10014, U.S.A.
Penguin Group (Canada), 90 Eglinton Avenue East, Suite 700,
Toronto, Ontario, Canada M4P 2Y3 (a division of Pearson Penguin Canada Inc.)
Penguin Books Ltd, 80 Strand, London WC2R ORL, England
Penguin Ireland, 25 St Stephen's Green, Dublin 2, Ireland (a division of Penguin Books Ltd)
Penguin Group (Australia), 250 Camberwell Road, Camberwell, Victoria 3124, Australia
(a division of Pearson Australia Group Pty Ltd)
Penguin Books India Pvt Ltd, 11 Community Centre,
Panchsheel Park, New Delhi - 110 017, India
Penguin Group (NZ), 67 Apollo Drive, Rosedale, North Shore 0632, New Zealand
(a division of Pearson New Zealand Ltd.)
Penguin Books (South Africa) (Pty) Ltd, 24 Sturdee Avenue,
Rosebank, Johannesburg 2196, South Africa

Registered Offices: Penguin Books Ltd, 80 Strand, London WC2R ORL, England

First published in the United States of America by G. P. Putnam's Sons,
a division of Penguin Young Readers Group, 2009
Published by Puffin Books, a division of Penguin Young Readers Group, 2010

7 9 10 8

THE LIBRARY OF CONGRESS HAS CATALOGED THE G. P. PUTNAM'S SONS EDITION AS FOLLOWS:
Pitchford, Dean.
Captain Nobody / by Dean Pitchford.
p. cm.
Summary: When ten-year-old Newton dresses up as an unusual superhero for Halloween,
he decides to keep wearing the costume after the holiday to help save townspeople and
eventually his injured brother.
ISBN 978-0-399-25034-7 (hc)
[1. Halloween—Fiction. 2. Brothers—Fiction. 3. Heroes—Fiction. 4. Self-confidence—Fiction.
5. Interpersonal relations—Fiction. 6. Costume—Fiction.] I. Title.
PZ7.P644Cap 2009 [Fic]—dc22 2008027733

Puffin Books ISBN 978-0-14-241667-9

Printed in the United States of America

Design by Richard Amari
Text set in Matt Antique

To Marie,

who taught me the power of words

CONTENTS

PROLOGUE *1*

1 IN WHICH NOBODY EATS BREAKFAST *3*

2 IN WHICH HALLOWEEN PLANS ARE MADE—
SORT OF *11*

3 IN WHICH I SEARCH FOR SOMEBODY I'M NOT *19*

4 IN WHICH FOOTBALL IS PLAYED AND
MISTAKES ARE MADE *26*

5 IN WHICH THE BAD DREAMS BEGIN *34*

6 IN WHICH I GET A TERRIBLE IDEA *44*

7 IN WHICH I HIDE—AND FIND MYSELF *54*

8 IN WHICH I RAISE MY VOICE *59*

9 IN WHICH I PRACTICE MY NEW NAME *63*

10 IN WHICH I MAKE A WILD
WARDROBE CHOICE *68*

11 IN WHICH CAPTAIN NOBODY FACES A FEAR *79*

12 IN WHICH CAPTAIN NOBODY FIRST
COMES TO THE RESCUE *85*

13 IN WHICH DAD MEETS CAPTAIN NOBODY *89*

14 IN WHICH CERTAIN THREATS ARE MADE *97*

15 IN WHICH BAD SPELLING LEADS TO
SOMETHING WORSE *104*

16 IN WHICH I DON'T APPEAR ON THE
FIVE O'CLOCK NEWS *112*

17 IN WHICH I CHEAT DEATH *120*

18 IN WHICH I LEARN AN
UNCOMFORTABLE TRUTH *134*

19 IN WHICH REGGIE RATNER
DECIDES TO END IT ALL *142*

20 IN WHICH I CLIMB UP TO THE SKY *149*

21 IN WHICH I FINISH FALLING *167*

22 IN WHICH I FINALLY GET
TO THE HOSPITAL *169*

23 IN WHICH I WAKE UP IN THE NEWS *182*

24 IN WHICH A LITTLE OLD LADY MAKES
ME LAUGH *190*

CAPTAIN
NOBODY

PROLOGUE

Uh-oh. This is not good.

I'm falling.

I'm not going to scream and yell about it, cuz I'm not the kind of kid who makes a lot of noise, but I'd like you to understand how critical my situation is. I—who am normally so terrified of heights that I avoid standing on tiptoe—I . . .

. . . am . . .

. . . *FALLING!*

A very, very long way.

How'd this happen? One moment, I was high above the ground, clinging to the rickety wooden ladder that runs up the side of Appleton's last remaining water tower, and in the next blink, my foot snapped through a rotted rung, my feet dropped out from under me and my hands lost their grip. I dropped backward—falling, falling, falling.

And I'm still going. Funny thing is, I'm not really scared. Maybe that'll come, but now, with all this time on my hands, I'm suddenly aware of a bazillion questions rocketing around inside my skull. Questions like:

Is the sky always this color, or does it just look so amazingly blue because I'm closer to it?

Did any of those firemen and police on the ground see me fall?

If they did, will they catch me?

If they don't, will it hurt when I land?

And if it does, will I have to go to school tomorrow?

But before I can answer any of those questions, they all get pushed aside, and my brain flips backward through a blizzard of pictures . . .

. . . and feelings . . .

. . . and smells . . .

. . . and moments . . .

. . . and the page-flipping stops—*screech!*

Yeah, I remember now.

It was the morning of the Big Game. The last time everything was okay.

1

IN WHICH
NOBODY EATS BREAKFAST

The sun wasn't up yet. It was the last Friday in October, so my breath made white puffs in the dark, cold air as I stepped out on the front porch to bring in the newspaper. In thick, black letters, the front page of the *Appleton Sentinel* announced, "Tonight's Big Game Is Biggest Yet!"

"You're not kidding," I muttered as I went back into the kitchen to start breakfast. Mom used to make it, but her phones usually start ringing by seven, and she gets distracted. One morning last year, after she poured milk into a bowl filled with strips of raw bacon, I offered to take over.

This particular morning, I got the Mr. Coffee brewing, and then I pulled the sports section from the paper. I almost whooped with surprise. There, at the top of the page, was a giant color photo of my big brother, Chris.

Chris Newman.

I know exactly what you're saying now: "Chris Newman? The football player? *Really?* I didn't know he had a brother!"

Yup. Chris Newman has a brother. A short, skinny, freckled, ten-year-old brother.

Newton Newman.

I'm not kidding. *Newton.* My parents swear that when they named me, they were thinking about the guy who discovered gravity and not about a fig cookie.

The article under my brother's picture began with a history of the Big Game and how it's been played for almost forty years between my brother's team, the Ferocious Ferrets of Fillmore High School, and their crosstown archenemies, the Chargers of Merrimac High.

Merrimac has always beat the pants off Fillmore. Always.

But two years ago, "while still an untested sophomore," the article said, "Chris Newman came off the bench to replace the quarterback in the last twenty seconds of the Big Game—with Fillmore five points behind. It was an electrifying debut."

I still get goose bumps when I remember the moment my brother took the snap. He backed up, looked around frantically for an open receiver, and when he couldn't find one, he put his head down . . .

. . . and plowed seventy-three yards down the field to deliver the first Fillmore victory against Merrimac. *Ever!*

"Last year, as a junior," read the last paragraph of the article, "Newman led the Ferrets to a second Big Game victory, and this year, with both teams undefeated, excitement is running high. Chris New-MANIA is sweeping the town!"

As I folded up the paper, I was smiling so hard my cheeks hurt. That's my big brother they were writing about!

I scrambled a platter of eggs and cooked up some sausages. The smells from the stove floated upstairs, and pretty soon, Dad came bounding down.

"G'mornin', kiddo," he said. "Smells good."

"Dad!" I grabbed the paper. "Check out what the *Sentinel* said about—"

Just then, Dad's cell phone rang, playing the Ferrets' fight song.

"Hang on, Newt," he said as he flipped the phone open.

My dad's the supervisor for a company that builds buildings all over the county—apartment houses and offices and places like that—so, in the weeks before the Big Game, before the first winds of November whip into Appleton and freeze the ground, Dad has to make sure that every hole that needs digging gets dug.

Dad started unrolling blueprints on the kitchen counter, so I just scooped eggs and sausages onto a plate, poured a cup of coffee, and set them down where he could reach them as he talked. I figured I'd tell him later about the article.

That's when Mom staggered in, lugging a sledgehammer and a dozen For Sale signs for the houses she would try to sell that day. "Sweetie," she mumbled, pecking me on the cheek, "did you see what I did with the keys to that three-bedroom on Elwood Street?"

I nodded toward the refrigerator. "Check behind the frozen waffles."

She looked startled. "Seriously?"

"Seriously."

Leaning the hammer and the wooden stakes against a wall, she opened the freezer and pulled out a frost-covered ring of keys. With a sigh, she dropped them into the pocket of her bathrobe. "I swear, Newt, if it weren't for you, I'd forget my head."

"Mom!" I waved the newspaper over my head. "You gotta see this morning's sports sec—" But that's when the kitchen phone rang. Mom held up a wait-a-second finger and plucked the receiver off the wall.

"Good morning! . . . Oh, hi, Carole. . . . Tonight's cookout? Well, if you've got a question, I've got an answer."

Since Chris's sports career took off, the number of family friends who show up for my parents' pregame tailgate barbecues has grown to the size of a small village. At first, Mom always takes charge and tells people what dishes to bring. But then she forgets.

"Newt," Mom said, holding the phone against her chest, "it's Carole Hennessey from across the street. Remind me—is she bringing a gallon of coleslaw or ice cream for thirty?"

"Mrs. Hennessey's in charge of potato chips," I said. "Ten bags."

"Of course!" she exclaimed and returned to her call. "Carole? I just remembered!"

She waved off the plate of food I'd prepared for her, but she cradled the phone to her shoulder so she could take the cup of coffee I'd poured. She sipped it as she walked around from room to room, stretching the phone cord to its limit.

Dad hadn't touched his food either, so I ate my breakfast, rereading the sports pages and waiting for Chris.

Ever since I'd started making breakfast for my family last year, Chris and I developed a little routine for whenever he'd oversleep. I would open his bedroom door and shout, "Hit the showers!" just the way I'd heard his coaches order over the years. Chris would usually mumble something and lob a pillow in my direction, but after a minute or two, he'd swing his legs out of bed.

The week before the Big Game, though, my parents stopped me from going upstairs. "Let him sleep," they'd say. "He's having a hard week."

After Fillmore beat Roosevelt Prep last Saturday night, Chris's team had only one day off before they

7

doubled up their workouts in preparation for the Big Game. Then after practice, Chris had to run around town doing interviews on the local TV and radio stations. And when he got home every night after the rest of us had finished eating, he took his dinner up to his bedroom and did his homework until late.

For almost all of last week, I didn't see him before I went to sleep. Finally, last night I caught him in the bathroom, where he was brushing his teeth.

"I bet you're really tired, huh, Chris?" I asked excitedly.

"Down to the bone," he sighed, before he rinsed and spit.

"I heard you on the radio."

"Oh, yeah?" He wiped his chin.

"You were awesome!"

"Thanks."

And then he was gone.

He wasn't being rude. He was just tired. I totally understand. But that's how it's been with us for a while now.

● ● ●

Dad interrupted his first phone call to jump on a second one and then another. He *still* hadn't touched his food. From time to time he'd motion for me to fetch him a pencil or to pour him more coffee. Mom wandered in and out, *still* talking to Mrs. Hennessey and peeking at the faxes that had started to curl out of the machine on her corner desk.

I stood at the stove, drumming my fingers in frustration. Pretty soon I'd have to leave for school, and I *still* hadn't shown Mom or Dad the newspaper article about Chris, and nobody had eaten my breakfast.

I looked down at what was left. The sausages were cooling in their grease. The eggs were getting watery. And I was getting . . . steamed.

I hardly ever get steamed.

Now, I realize there's really not a lot I can do to help my family as they whiz through their busy days. And maybe I don't build buildings or win ball games. *But if I make breakfast, the least they can do is eat it!*

Since Mom and Dad were still on the phone, I focused all my frustration on Chris. Ignoring their instruction to "let your brother sleep," I dropped my spatula, stormed upstairs and threw open his bedroom door.

"Hit the showers!" I barked.

As usual, Chris mumbled, "I'mupI'mup," and tossed a pillow my way. But it wasn't enough to wake him. When he started to snore again, I hit the roof.

"HIT THE SHOWERS!" I bellowed, louder than I'd ever bellowed before.

Startled, Chris jerked his head up and looked around through half-closed eyes. "Stop yelling," he growled sleepily, and, with all the strength of a star quarterback, he threw another pillow at me. The force of his

9

throw, however, made him roll forward, and in an avalanche of sheets and blankets, he tumbled out of bed. *THUD!*—he hit the floor hard.

Then my big brother—who's always getting tackled by monster football players and never complains—whimpered one high-pitched, teensy word.

"Ow."

I couldn't help myself. I started to laugh.

"Not funny, bro," Chris grunted, which only made me laugh harder. Which only upset Chris more.

He struggled to his feet, and wearing only a pair of gym shorts, he chased me down the stairs, through the kitchen and out into the backyard.

That's where I turned the garden hose on him.

When the freezing water hit his bare skin, Chris's eyes finally flew open. He waved his arms in frantic surrender and shrieked, "I'm up! I'm up!"

Still holding their phones, Mom and Dad came dashing out of the house, mouths open in astonishment.

"Now," I said quietly, "who wants breakfast?"

2

IN WHICH
HALLOWEEN
PLANS ARE MADE—
SORT OF

When I got to school that morning, the playground at Appleton Elementary was packed with kids running around, punching each other, and shrieking as usual. I took a deep breath and squeezed my way through the crowds. Whenever I saw one of my classmates, I waved and quietly said, "How's it going?" like I do every morning.

And like they do every morning, they looked right through me.

I plopped down on a large boulder at the far end of the school yard, sharpened a pencil and began to draw in my Secret Superhero Sketchbook.

• • •

When I was really small, Chris would sit me in his lap and read to me from his humongous collection of comic books. Even though I was too young to understand the stories, I was hypnotized by the pictures of the super-heroes with their awesome powers. As soon as I could hold a pencil, I spent hours on the floor of Chris's bedroom, carefully tracing the characters in his comics. When I got a little older, I began to invent my own.

My first sketches were pretty crummy, but eventually my scrawls began to take shape. First I created Master Key, a crimefighter whose hands could transform into keys that could open any lock in existence. After that came Paper Boy, who could flatten his body until it was so thin that he could slip under any door. Since then, I've filled dozens of Secret Superhero Sketchbooks, but I've never shown my drawings to anyone.

Except JJ and Cecil, of course.

● ● ●

Juanita Josephina Gonzalez—JJ for short—is the tallest girl in the fourth grade, and with a head full of thick, untamed black hair, she cast a very recognizable shadow over my sketchbook.

"Hey, JJ," I said without looking up.

"Hey, Newt." She leaned over my shoulder and studied the picture. "Ooh, I like this one. What's his name?"

"Wait, wait, wait!" Cecil Butterworth shouted, racing across the playground. "Don't tell the story yet!"

Cecil is the only kid in our class who is shorter and skinnier than I am, but what he lacks in size he makes up for in volume. Once he joined us, Cecil clapped his hands and said, "All right, let's have it! Who's today's superfreak?"

"I'm calling this one Guy Wire. He used to be a wimpy librarian, but after he was exposed to radiation from a meteorite, he discovered that he could stretch his arms and fingers and legs into steel wires and do cool things like turn his legs into springs and bounce anywhere he wants to go."

"Sweet!" laughed Cecil.

"Highly commendable." JJ nodded.

"Highly *what*?" Cecil raised an eyebrow. "Lady, sometimes I swear you swallowed a dictionary."

JJ taught herself to read at the age of three with the help of a wooden alphabet puzzle and a really big brain. She hasn't stopped reading ever since.

"'Commendable' just means deserving of praise," JJ explained. "Like Newt's drawing."

"Well, I think it deserves a drumroll." Cecil pulled two drumsticks out of his backpack and did a quick rat-a-tat on the rock where I was sitting.

Cecil's dream is to be a drummer, but until his parents break down, get earplugs and buy Cecil a drum set of his own, he's determined to practice every chance he gets.

Cecil finished his drum solo with a crash—*bish!*—and then announced, "Okay, listen up! Does anybody remember what this weekend is?"

"Please!" I exclaimed. "It's the weekend of the Big Game."

He shook his head. "I'm talking about Sunday."

JJ and I shared a shrug.

"Hello?" Cecil waved his arms about. "Can anybody say 'Halloween'?"

"Really?" I said. "This Sunday?"

Ever since we met in first grade, JJ, Cecil and I have always trick-or-treated together, but I guess I'd been so wrapped up in my brother's final Big Game that Halloween had slipped my mind.

"Y'know what, guys?" JJ twirled a strand of hair around a finger and squidged up her nose. "I'm bored with Halloween."

"Bored with Halloween?" Cecil yelped. "I got two words for you: Free. Candy."

"Oh, c'mon, we're in fourth grade now," JJ insisted. "We've outgrown candy."

"Now you're just talking crazy," Cecil scoffed.

That made me laugh; Cecil can always make me laugh.

"And besides," JJ added, "our costumes suck. They always have."

We all nodded glumly. See, the three of us have always been forced to wear hand-me-downs. Like her four sisters before her, JJ had been a flamenco dancer twice, a Starbucks countergirl once, and last year she was Jennifer Lopez. Cecil always wears the same old Wolverine mask that his brothers had gotten so much use out of. And the first year we all went trick-or-treating together, my mom completely forgot that it was Halloween, so at the last minute I searched through the stacks of plastic storage bins in our garage until I found Chris's old cowboy suit. I've been a cowboy ever since.

"I refuse to be J. Lo again," JJ moaned.

"My Wolverine mask is falling apart," Cecil griped.

"And my cowboy pants have split," I sighed.

After a gloomy moment of silence, Cecil looked up. "Y'know what's wrong with us?"

"I didn't realize there was something wrong," I said.

"Me neither," JJ said. "But if there was, what would it be?"

Cecil swept his arms to indicate the hundreds of kids at play. "To everybody in this school, we are invisible."

"I don't think you actually mean *invisible*," JJ corrected him, "because our bodies *do* have mass, and they *do* reflect light."

"Okay, everybody *ignores* us, then." Cecil turned to me. "Doesn't it bother you how kids are always stepping on us in the hallways, almost like we aren't there?"

"We're both really short," I suggested.

"And, JJ," Cecil went on, "how does it make you feel when people shove you away from the water fountain . . ."

"That's only happened eight or nine times," she said quietly.

". . . or what about in the cafeteria when they slide our food off the table and squeeze us out of our seats?"

JJ and I exchanged a look. He had a point.

"Nobody pays any attention to us any other day of the year," Cecil declared, waving a finger overhead as if he were preaching. "And I say that Halloween's the one night we get to say, 'Look at me! Look at me!' And y'know what? People will."

"Why?" I asked. "Who're we gonna be?"

"Anybody we want," Cecil said firmly.

JJ shook her head. "I don't think you actually mean *anybody*. There are only a limited number of character costumes manufactured each year, and—"

"I'm not talking about some costume in a box at Walmart! Shrek? Heck! Darth Vader? See ya later! I say we get personal. We gotta dig deep down inside and find our inner . . . *other*."

"Our inner *other*?" JJ snorted. Despite her large vocabulary and extensive knowledge of books, JJ is generally suspicious about new ideas. Especially Cecil's.

"Yeah! Our *inner other* is who we *would* be if we didn't have to be *us*." Cecil was on a roll now. "Think of it like a . . . a personal hero."

"What if I don't have one?" I asked. "A personal hero, I mean."

"We've all got one." Cecil whipped around to JJ. "You! Isn't there anybody in those books you're always reading, somebody witchy and wonderful you secretly wish you could be for one night?"

Cecil's question caught JJ by surprise. Ever since she read a ten-part epic called *The Crystal Cavern Chronicles*, JJ has been hopelessly hooked on stories about witches, wizards and dragons.

"I don't know . . . maybe," she stuttered.

"Maybe?" Cecil taunted. "That's not the JJ I know."

"Well, okay, Mr. Motivation," JJ fired back. "Who would you be?"

"Yeah. Who's your hero, Cecil?" I asked.

"Me?" Cecil squinted until a thought hit him, and he smiled. "Music! Music's my hero."

JJ frowned. "But you can't dress up as *music*."

"Who says?" Cecil threw up his hands. "I can wrap myself in sheet music and come as a symphony!"

"What about you, Newt?" JJ asked. "Who's your inner other?"

"Yeah, you're always whippin' up those crazy cool crimefighters," Cecil said, pointing to my Secret Superhero Sketchbook. "Which one of them is you?"

I flipped through my drawing pad, but nothing caught my eye.

"I . . . I have to give it some thought" was all I could manage.

"Okay, how's this?" Cecil's eyes were sparkling. "We've got three days. We make our own costumes, and then, on Halloween night, we surprise each other."

JJ still seemed nervous. "But even if I knew who I wanted to be . . . ," she stammered, "let's just say . . . where . . . I mean, how do we get the clothes?"

"Oh, right. Where *do* we?" I wondered.

"Where's your imagination, people?" Cecil cried. "Are these not the top three minds in the fourth grade?"

We shrugged in agreement.

JJ started again, "But what if I can't—"

Cecil held a finger up to her lips just as the first bell rang. "Hup! Zip it!" he ordered. "No more 'can't,' 'don't,' 'won't.' We're gonna think positive, heroic thoughts. And in three days, we're gonna have our own Halloween parade. Whaddya say?"

JJ and I smiled at each other as we gathered up our stuff and headed to class.

"That'd be so cool," I said. "Let's do it for us."

"For us," JJ echoed.

"*And*," shouted Cecil, "for the free candy!"

IN WHICH
I SEARCH FOR
SOMEBODY I'M NOT

All through class that morning, Cecil's questions rang in my ears. *Who is my inner other? Do I have a personal hero?* Every time we switched to a new subject, I desperately looked for an answer.

In social studies, before our teacher Mrs. Young did a slide show about the gods and goddesses of ancient Rome and Greece, she called them "the heroes of old." I sat up, thinking, *Wow! Isn't that what I'm looking for?*

I imagined myself as Zeus, god of lightning. Or maybe Neptune, who ruled the seas. I mean, who wouldn't want to hurl thunderbolts or control the waves?

But once Mrs. Young projected their pictures on the

screen, I lost my nerve. In slide after slide, these guys were massive, muscley *giants*. Giants in white robes with flowing beards. Even if I could whip up a white robe and glue on a beard, where was I going to get the muscles?

Forget that.

During American History, I got excited by the stories of the pioneers who crossed the dangerous frontier and built our country with their bare hands. "If those people aren't heroes," I said to myself, "I don't know who are."

I raised my hand. "Yes, Newt?" Mrs. Young responded.

"Mrs. Young, what did the pioneers wear?"

Behind me, Bobby Asher—who insists on being called "Basher"—snorted, "Clothes, you jerk!" A dozen other kids laughed.

"Newt has a good question," Mrs. Young said, shooting a look at Basher. "In the early days of America, the pioneers didn't always have fabric, so they used whatever was available. Sometimes it was animal skins or furs, but if they were desperate, they might make clothes from birds' feathers or even tree bark."

Feathers and tree bark?

I started to itch. And scratch. Clearly, I wasn't cut out to be a pioneer. I'd have to keep looking.

• • •

That day, school let out early so we could line the street—like everyone else in town—and watch the Big Game Pep Parade go by.

Since Fillmore won last year's game, their band marched past first, trumpeting and drumming up a storm. Behind them came their football players, waving from the backseats of convertibles.

JJ, Cecil and I stood together at the back of the crowd. Cecil and I couldn't see much over all the people in front of us, but JJ assured me that my big brother was waving and smiling from the front car.

Next, the Fillmore Spirit Squad rolled past on the back of a long flatbed truck, clapping and screaming over a PA system.

"WHO'S GONNA MASSACRE MERRIMAC?" *Clap, clap.* "WE ARE!" *Clap, clap.* "WE ARE!" *Clap, clap.* Because Cecil can never resist a rhythm, he clapped along with the cheerleaders.

Suddenly JJ groaned. "Ugh! Do you believe that?" She wagged a finger at a truck going by.

I craned my neck to see what was upsetting her. A banner stretched across the Spirit Squad truck said, BEHOLD THE FEROCIOUS FIGHTING FERRET'S OF FILLMORE!

"Why did they have to put an apostrophe in Ferrets?" JJ exploded. "It's not possessive. It's *plural.* F-E-R-R-E-T-no apostrophe-S." She shook her head in dismay. "I wish they would ask me before they paint these mistakes four feet high."

"Hey," I said, "are you guys coming to the game tonight?"

"How can we?" Cecil threw his hands in the air. "My uncle tried getting tickets last week, and they told him the Big Game has been sold out since August!"

"And did you know," JJ said, "that people are auctioning tickets online for, like, four hundred dollars *apiece*?"

"Wow," I said.

"Besides," JJ continued, "I have tons to do if I'm ever going to be ready for Halloween."

Cecil's eyes widened. "So you know who you're gonna be?"

"Maybe," JJ smiled mysteriously. "Don't you?"

"Are you kidding?" Cecil scoffed, tapping the side of his head. "I got my whole thing planned from head to foot. And Newt, how're you doing?"

"Yeah," JJ asked excitedly. "Did you make a decision?"

I looked at their expectant faces and shrugged. "Oh, y'know. I'm weighing a couple possibilities."

JJ nudged Cecil with her elbow. "Bet you he's already got the whole thing drawn up in his Secret Sketchbook."

"Course he has! And y'know why?" Cecil winked, still clapping along with the cheerleaders. "Because he's Newt!" *Clap, clap.* "Newt!" *Clap, clap.* "Newt!" *Clap, clap.* "The Newt-ron bomb!"

I smiled weakly as a bead of nervous sweat rolled from my right armpit to my waist.

• • •

I raced home from school and pulled out a stack of my old Secret Superhero Sketchbooks from my closet. I hoped I might find inspiration from one of the characters I had created over the years. But with every page flip, that hope faded.

For one thing, most of my heroes stretch and transform their bodies into fantastic shapes. Tommy Origami, for instance, can fold his body into a packet the size of a postage stamp.

Who was I kidding? I can barely touch my toes.

And even if I *did* dress up as one of my sketches, I'd have to explain who I was to everyone I met. After all, nobody but Cecil and JJ have ever even heard of Dwight, The Mighty Termite, who can chew his way through a wood wall in ten seconds. Or what about Gas Man, who can empty a shopping mall full of people just by . . . well, never mind.

I went online and Googled "hero." The first thing that came up was the headline "Hero Saves Stranger from Sharks."

"Whoa!" I clicked on the link.

The story was about a lady who was taking a sightseeing tour in San Francisco Bay when she fell overboard into a school of sharks. Before they could eat her, though, another tourist—a guy who didn't even know her!—jumped in the freezing water, punched one shark in the snout, poked another one in the eye and pulled the lady to safety.

The man who saved her was interviewed, and when he was asked if he considered himself a hero, he said, "Heck. I'm just the guy next door."

Maybe that's the kind of hero I have inside, I thought. *Not a shape-shifter or a pioneer, but an everyday, guy-next-door kind of hero.*

I was getting all excited about this idea until I scrolled down to a picture of the shark-puncher. He turned out to be a skinny guy in blue jeans. His wet hair was plastered to his forehead and his dripping T-shirt read, I ♥ KETCHUP.

Uh-oh, I thought. *If I wear that, how will people know I'm a hero?*

With a groan, I laid my head down on my arms. I must have fallen asleep for a moment, because the next thing I knew, I was having a terrible dream in which I was trick-or-treating on my block. When a neighbor answered her door and asked, "Who are you supposed to be, little boy?" I looked down to see my costume only to find that . . . *I was totally naked!*

I woke up panting like a racehorse.

Downstairs I heard Mom and Dad loading up their SUVs with supplies for the pregame cookout.

"Newt!" Mom yelled up. "Where did I put the plastic forks?"

"You left them in the guest bathroom," I called down. "I'll get them."

With a heavy heart, I turned off my computer and put my Secret Superhero Sketchbooks back in the closet. My search for my inner other was going to have to wait.

It was time for the Big Game.

4

IN WHICH
FOOTBALL IS PLAYED AND MISTAKES ARE MADE

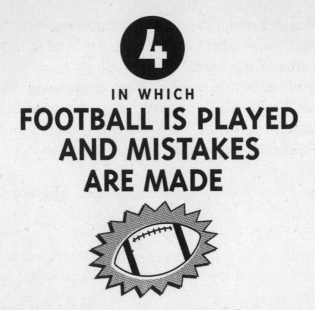

That night, so many people showed up for my parents' tailgate barbecue in the stadium parking lot that in just a half hour we ran out of hot dog buns. And coleslaw. And napkins.

"It's Chris Newman's last football game!" shouted our neighbor Mr. Hennessey between bites of his cheeseburger. "We wouldn't have missed it for the world!"

As Dad worked the grill, he kept checking his pager and answering his ever-ringing cell phone. "Come on down!" he told everyone who called. "The more the merrier."

While arranging trays of chips and dips, my mother muttered, "I wish I could remember where I put the egg rolls."

"Mom," I said, "they already ate the egg rolls."

"Well, no wonder I can't find them!" She sighed. "I was afraid I was losing my mind."

I carried the chip trays through the growing crowd. Most folks helped themselves without interrupting their conversations. Once in a while, though, someone would look down and notice me. Then they'd all ask the same question.

"Hey, Newt! You must be so excited for your brother, huh?"

"Yeah. Real excited. You want a chip?"

And I *was* excited. I swear. But I couldn't shake the feeling that I should be home, making a costume for Sunday night.

At seven o'clock, the Fillmore High School marching band paraded through the parking lot and into the jam-packed stadium. We shut down the barbecue, loaded all the picnic stuff into my parents' SUVs and took our seats.

As usual, my mom and dad had reserved a section halfway up the bleachers on the fifty-yard line where they could be surrounded by tons of neighbors and friends. I had a ticket for a seat somewhere in the middle of that mob, but as more and more people crammed in around Mom and Dad—hugging and chatting and eating and drinking—I found myself being squeezed out of my place, squished down the row, and squashed onto an end seat next to a very large lady, who jumped to her feet and shrieked like a fire engine during the opening kickoff. When she sat back down without looking where she was going, she just about flattened me. I scooted sideways in the nick of time . . .

. . . and landed—*splat!*—in the aisle.

I didn't really feel like fighting my way back to my seat. Halloween was still on my mind, so I wandered down the aisle and leaned against a railing. I watched the game with glazed eyes, worried that I was totally going to disappoint my only two friends in the world.

But then things began to happen on the field that made me forget my Halloween blues.

For three years in a row, the #1 defensive end in the county has been this guy from Merrimac High named Reggie Ratner. Reggie weighs about two hundred and eighty pounds and has a neck as thick as a telephone pole. My brother used to joke, "Reggie Ratner looks like a concrete truck with hair." In the two previous years' games, Reggie had chased my brother all over the field, but he'd never been able to bring Chris down, *not once!* So the day before this year's Big Game, the headline in the *Appleton Sentinel* asked, "Will Ratner Finally Get Revenge?" In the article, Reggie was quoted as saying, "You watch. I'm gonna snap Chris Newman like a day-old breadstick."

From the opening drive, it looked like Reggie was determined to keep his promise. The Fillmore Ferrets tried their best to control him, but time after time Reggie broke through two, three, even four Ferrets and charged after my brother. In every case, though, Chris was able to hand off the ball or pass it at the last possible second. Reggie actually got so frustrated at one point that he yanked off his helmet and smashed it to the ground.

"Crybaby! Crybaby!" yelled the Fillmore fans.

"Crush him, Reggie!" shrieked the Merrimac fans.

It went on like that, with both teams bashing each other senseless for the first two quarters. Fortunately, as the halftime horn sounded, the Fillmore Ferrets were leading, 21–14.

When the crowds stood up to stretch their legs, I blinked and looked around, confused. Without realizing it, I had gotten so caught up in the action that I had followed the game up and down the field, pacing in the aisles. Now I found myself standing at the far end of the bleachers. I sat down on a step and tried to use halftime to focus on my Halloween costume problem.

Suddenly from behind me a voice boomed, "Can I see your ticket?"

I turned to find a tubby, red-faced teenager wearing a Fillmore Ferrets button pinned on his Fillmore HS Usher jacket.

"Excuse me?" I said.

"You can't sit here," the teen barked. "There's rules."

I scrambled to my feet. "Oh. See, you're gonna laugh. . . . I'm actually supposed to be over there"—I pointed to the midfield seats—"but I kinda got squeezed out . . ."

"Ticket!" The usher snapped his fingers in my face.

"It's here somewhere," I promised, digging deeper and deeper into my empty pockets.

And that's how I wound up standing out in the parking lot at the far end of the stadium, watching the second half through the wire fence surrounding Fillmore Field.

• • •

When the Ferrets stormed back from their locker room, I positioned myself so I could look between the uprights of the goalpost, right down the middle of the field. It was weird seeing the game from that angle because, depending on the play, the teams were either running away from me . . . or directly at me. For the first time ever, I truly understood the scary stampede my brother was always facing.

As I stood on the cold, wet grass in the dark, the Ferrets and the Chargers battled through the third quarter and into the fourth. My brother was doing a fantastic job of keeping Fillmore out in front until—with only *forty-five seconds left to play in the game*—Merrimac kicked a field goal and pulled ahead by two points. The enemy was winning!

I paced nervously as Merrimac kicked off to Fillmore for the last time. A few more plays brought the Ferrets far enough downfield toward me that I could now see Chris huddling with his team through the backs of the Charger defense. But I could also see the clock.

It said :07.

"No way!" I gasped. Chris only had enough time for one more play! It was his *last* chance to save his *final* game.

The Ferrets lined up opposite the Merrimac defense. Time slowed to a painful crawl, and it seemed like it took forever for my brother to bark his signals and take the snap.

Then everything exploded into fast motion.

As Reggie Ratner bulldozed through the line, Chris staggered backward, looking for a receiver. Reggie lunged for my brother, but Chris faked to one side and left him grabbing at empty air. Chris spun around and handed the ball off to Darryl Peeps, his running back, who found a hole and started tearing down the field. The screaming in the bleachers sounded like ten jet engines at full throttle, and I swear I was screaming louder than all of them.

The Merrimac players looked like an orange-and-green avalanche roaring toward me, while on all sides, red-and-white Ferrets chased anybody who got close to Darryl. At the fifteen-yard line, a Merrimac tackle lunged for Darryl and caught one ankle.

"No!" I shrieked. "Stay up! Stay up!"

Just as Darryl tumbled to the turf, he tossed the ball sideways—*right into the hands of my big brother,* who, as usual, was in just the right place at the right time.

The stadium went *wild!*

Please don't think I'm a wuss when I tell you that tears welled up in my eyes as my brother zigged and zagged, dodging tackle after tackle in the last ten!, nine!, eight! yards. Everyone was closing in, surrounding Chris in a tidal wave of green-and-orange-and-red-and-white. And leading the pack, breathing down my brother's neck, was Reggie Ratner.

Finally, at the two-yard line, a desperate Merrimac player dove right across my brother's path. I shrieked, "Chris, watch out!" But he didn't need my advice. In the next split second, my brother extended the ball in his outstretched hands and, with a flying leap, sailed over that Charger and crossed the goal line.

TOUCHDOWN!

Immediately both teams buried my brother in a thunderous *crash!* of shoulder pads and *crack!* of helmets that was louder than anything I had ever heard from up in the bleachers. But it didn't matter.

Fillmore had won!

The Fillmore stands erupted with confetti and streamers, and the Ferrets' marching band tore into the school fight song. Cheerleaders waving victory banners ran up and down the field as miniature cannons boomed.

In the Merrimac bleachers, people covered their

faces and sobbed. Along the sidelines, the rest of the Chargers' football team bowed their heads in disappointment.

The crying and cheering continued until the players had all untangled and peeled themselves off the pile.

All but one.

And in the time it takes a heart to beat, every sound stopped.

5

IN WHICH
THE BAD DREAMS BEGIN

From my place behind the fence, I saw everything that happened next. Coach Gavin and the Fillmore assistant coaches rushed into the end zone, pushing through the players to huddle over my brother. They kept repeating, "Chris! Hey, buddy! Can you hear me?" until four or five adults from the bleachers joined them. Each one announced, "I'm a doctor!" as they ran up, and then *they* took turns kneeling over Chris and calling his name.

An ambulance rolled onto the field just as Mom and Dad arrived. The doctors and the coaches shook their heads with concern and said some stuff that I couldn't hear. Mom covered her mouth with one hand, and Dad put his arm around her shoulder.

"What did they say?" I wanted to shout, but my mouth was dry, and I didn't have the breath to make a sound.

The ambulance guys put my brother on a backboard and lifted him onto a rolling stretcher. While both teams stood by with their helmets in hand, Chris was wheeled into the ambulance as my mother climbed in alongside him. Everything was so quiet that, even from where I stood, I could hear Dad say to Mom, "I'll meet you at the hospital."

Not a single person in the stadium moved until the wailing siren faded in the distance, and then the crowd filed out in stunned silence. It took me a moment before I snapped to and realized that I couldn't stand there all night.

I ran across the crowded parking lot to where Dad was backing out.

"Newt! Where've you been?" he asked, rolling down his window. "We looked everywhere for you at halftime."

"I lost my ticket," I panted, "but I saw what happened to Chris. How is he?"

"He's unconscious," said Dad, rubbing his eyes. "That's all we know right now." His cell phone was ringing, but he didn't answer it. "Listen, I'm going to join your mom at the hospital."

"Can I come?" I asked quickly.

"It's gonna be crowded," Dad said. "Dr. Snow and

Dr. Stanford—they were sitting with us, remember? They're going to meet us there."

"How come they get to go?" I asked.

"Because they're his doctors."

"But I'm his brother!"

"I know, kiddo." Dad nodded. "But until we know how serious this is . . ." Dad's voice caught in his throat. He sniffled and tried to start again. "Until we get a better idea of what's happened to your brother—"

"It's okay, Dad," I interrupted him. I could see how hard this was on him. I wasn't making it any easier.

He smiled and quietly said, "Thank you." Then he looked past me and called, "Carole? Stephen?"

Mr. and Mrs. Hennessey were walking to their car. They turned at the sound of my dad's voice.

"Can you drive Newt home?"

"Absolutely!" Mrs. Hennessy told my dad, putting an arm around my shoulder. "You go see Chris. We'll take care of Newt."

"I appreciate it, Carole." Dad looked at me. "I'll call you from the hospital, kiddo. And don't worry," he said before he drove off, "your brother's got a hard head. I'm sure he's gonna be fine."

● ● ●

And Dad was right. Sort of.

"Nothing's broken. Nothing's sprained," Dad sighed with relief when he finally called me at eleven o'clock that night. "And they're doing every kind of test: a CAT scan, X-rays, the works."

"Then what's wrong with him?" I asked.

"Well, he's . . ." Dad hesitated. "He's in a coma, Newt."

"That's bad, huh?"

"Maybe. Maybe not," Dad said carefully. He was quick to add, "His brain's healthy, and his spinal cord is fine. He's just . . . *out.*"

"He's been working real hard. Maybe he just needs the rest?" I suggested.

Dad chuckled. "Well, that's a good way to think of it. I'll tell your mother that. It'll cheer her up."

"When can I see him?" I asked.

There was a long pause before Dad said, "Can we figure that out later?"

"Sure," I answered, trying not to let my voice betray the disappointment I felt.

"So, here's the deal," Dad said. "One of us is going to stay here, and one of us will come home. But you get yourself to bed. Can you do that?"

Before I could answer, there was a beep on the phone, and I knew what was coming.

"Oops, there's my other line," Dad grumbled. "Gotta go."

"Okay, but, Dad, what if Chris—" I started to ask, but then I heard the line go dead.

● ● ●

When I was really young and still afraid of the dark, Chris would lean into my room at bedtime, and just before he clicked off the light he'd say, "Oh, by the way, bro, there's a monster under your bed." Even though I'd wail, "Chris, don't do that!" the sound of my brother laughing quietly out in the hall somehow made me feel I had nothing to be afraid of.

I lay awake that night, staring at my bedroom door, trying to imagine that Chris was just outside, good as new, chuckling like he used to. But each time I closed my eyes, my brain replayed Chris's touchdown—the blur of bodies . . . the crunch of shoulder pads . . . the crack of helmets. As soon as the noises stopped, the memory rewound. The players' bodies flew up off the pile and their legs pumped furiously, carrying them backward to the twenty-yard line. Then the whole thing started again.

Blur! Crunch! Crack! Rewind!

Blur! Crunch! Crack! . . .

Yikes!

I sat up, punched my pillow and tried to focus on something else. I stared at the shadow of tree branches scratching on my bedroom ceiling, which reminded me of monster claws. Which reminded me of . . .

Halloween!

My stomach cramped.

"Come on, Newt," I moaned in the dark. "You've got two days. Who's your personal hero?"

Instead of counting sheep, I ticked off heroic names

and occupations in my head: "Fireman? Who'm I kidding? Christopher Columbus? Wasn't he fat? Astronaut? Ha-ha."

Eventually, I drifted off. The next thing I knew, Mom was shaking me awake.

"Newt, honey?"

I opened one eye and asked sleepily, "How is he?"

"Your brother's vital signs are good, and he's resting comfortably. So . . ." She shrugged.

"Oh." I was relieved that Mom didn't sound worried—just tired. "So, Mom. You want some breakfast?"

"Oh, no. I'll get something at the hospital. Your father spent the night there, but he'll come back sometime today." She folded and stacked the clothes that I had tossed off on my way to bed. "There's orange juice in the fridge, and I got you some sliced turkey for lunch." Her eyes narrowed with confusion. "Or it might be sliced chicken. Whatever. It's sliced."

She looked at me. "Are you going to be okay on your own?"

"Mom," I groaned. "I'm ten."

She leaned down and kissed me on the head. "I forget sometimes."

I wasn't totally awake, or else I would have asked a lot more questions before she left the room. Anything to get her to stay and talk a little longer.

● ● ●

All day Saturday the phone rang. I knew most of the callers, but some were total strangers who were just anxious for any news about my brother. I wrote down all the messages and answered every question as best I could without alarming anybody.

"My dad says that nothing's broken."

"My mom says he's resting comfortably."

"Nah, don't send flowers. . . . *'Why?'* Cuz his eyes are closed."

JJ and Cecil dropped by that afternoon. They each brought me a CD to cheer me up. JJ gave me a recording of some famous English actor reading the first Harry Potter book.

"He pronounces every word correctly," she pointed out. "I smile every time I listen to it."

"And this here's *The Battle of the Drums*," Cecil announced, handing me his gift. "It's one smashin', bashin' drum solo after another. But you don't want to listen to it through earphones, cuz this stuff'll scramble your brain."

"Thanks, you guys," I said. I looked from JJ to Cecil, who were both watching me with concern.

"Oh!" I suddenly understood. "You're worried that I'm worried."

"You're not?" JJ asked skeptically.

"No, not at all. And y'know why?"

"No, why?" JJ echoed.

"Because Chris is gonna be okay. He really is."

They both nodded, and I nodded back, but we all seemed to have temporarily run out of words. So it was a relief when Cecil smacked his thigh and exclaimed, "Man! Whatever happened in that stadium last night is all anybody's talking about this morning. It was all over the news."

"My sister told me that people are phoning into radio programs like crazy," added JJ. "They're already calling it the Big Tackle."

"They even canceled the Victory Parade," said Cecil.

"You're not serious!" I cried. Each year the school that wins the Big Game gets their very own parade, which is way bigger and better than the Pep Parade. It never occurred to me that anything—not even my brother's tackle—could interfere with that tradition.

"It's true," JJ chimed in. "The principal of Fillmore High School said that the Ferrets won't celebrate until your brother's there to celebrate with them."

I shook my head. "Wow."

"And just be glad you're not that guy . . . what's his name . . . ?" Cecil snapped his fingers to help him remember.

"Who?" I asked.

"That defensive end from Merrimac," JJ explained. "Reggie Ratner."

"Yeah, he's the one," Cecil said. "That dude is screwed!"

"Why?" I asked. "What did Reggie do?"

"Everybody's saying he's the one who head-butted your brother after the touchdown," said Cecil. "Knocked him out colder than an ice cube."

"Apparently the two of them had some sort of rivalry going?" JJ asked.

"And this morning, at like three A.M., a bunch of players from your brother's school went to this Ratner guy's house," Cecil said excitedly. "They spray painted his car and slashed his tires."

"That's terrible!" I yelped. I strained to remember what I had seen the night before. Was it really Reggie who rammed into my brother's helmet? Or was it another player? There were so many bodies and it all happened so fast and—

"So!" JJ announced, the way she always does when she wants to change the subject. "What time should we start tomorrow night?"

"Oh, baby baby baby!" Cecil grinned broadly and swiveled his hips in a little dance move he calls the "Cecil Seesaw." "You guys are not *ready* for what I've got planned!"

My throat tightened. "Uh . . . I don't know. Tomorrow night's maybe not the best time for me to leave the house."

Cecil looked out of the kitchen, through the empty dining room and into the deserted living room. "Oh, yeah. I can see you've got lots going on here."

"Moping around isn't going to make Chris come around any faster," JJ said gently.

Cecil added, "And you say you can't go to the hospital, so . . ."

"So?" I asked.

"So!" JJ declared, standing. "Six o'clock it is."

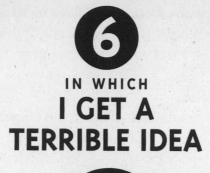

IN WHICH
I GET A
TERRIBLE IDEA

After JJ and Cecil left, I tore the house apart, desperate to find some idea—*any idea*—for my Halloween costume. I looked through all the DVDs in the den, searching for inspiration from a screen hero. I paged through books and magazines, and I switched on every TV—upstairs and downstairs—hoping that I might hear or see something that would make me shout, "Yes! *That's* my inner other!"

It didn't happen.

By the time I heated a can of SpaghettiOs for dinner, I was feeling awfully low. My dad called at ten-thirty to tell me not to wait up, but just as I started to ask him about Chris, a doctor came into the waiting room, and Dad had to hang up.

I put the phone next to my bed in case he called back, and I fell asleep watching *Saturday Night Live*.

● ● ●

When I was four, Chris taught me to skate on my grandparents' frozen pond. In the dream I had that night, we were back there again. I felt my brother holding me up as I stumbled and slid, shivering from the cold but determined to learn what Chris was teaching me. I couldn't remember ever being so happy. But then, just as Chris gave a gentle shove that sent me gliding smoothly across the ice, I heard a noise like thundering cattle. I looked back to find that we were now . . .

. . . on the football field in the last seconds of the Big Game. Chris was in his uniform, standing in the path of the stampeding teams. In the next second, with a blur of colors and a blitz of body parts, the world crashed down on my brother while I stood by and watched, helpless.

I woke up with a jolt. After a few blinks, I realized that it was already Sunday morning. From my bedroom window I saw Dad's car in the driveway. My first thought was *He'll need some breakfast!* Sitting down to eat with my dad—just the two of us—was such an exciting plan that I raced downstairs to scramble eggs and brown some sausages.

Just as everything was about ready, Dad bolted through the kitchen. "Hey! I bet you're hungry, huh?" I called out.

"Oh, hey, kiddo," Dad said as he grabbed his car keys. "I told your mom I'd eat with her at the hospital. Then she'll be back later this afternoon." The beeper on his belt buzzed. "Oh, great," he said, and raced out.

I chased him through the laundry room and out to the driveway.

"Wait, Dad! What's happening with Chris?"

"Well, his blood tests are back. They're all good," Dad explained, climbing into his car. "His heart scan's good. Breathing's good. Everything's good." He started the car and backed down the driveway, calling out, "Now all we can do is wait."

• • •

I went out to pick up the *Sunday Appleton Sentinel* off the porch. On the front page, above an amazing photo of Chris flying through the air on his way to that winning touchdown, was the headline: "Newman's Bittersweet Victory." The article was about my brother's first day in the hospital, but it was the second paragraph that made me catch my breath.

"Chris Newman," it read, "the only child of Patrick and Mary Newman of Appleton . . ."

The only child?

I turned the paper over and left it on the washing machine.

As I ate breakfast, I listened to Cecil's CD of drum solos. It was very energetic. It even got me tapping my foot, although I'm sure I was nowhere near the beat.

All that noise and energy lifted my spirits, and I began to think that maybe . . . maybe I could still save Halloween. Maybe it wasn't too late. Maybe any old costume would be better than no costume at all.

I dug through bins and boxes in the garage again until I found my old cowboy outfit. But it was worse than I remembered: the pants were torn and way too short. The hat was crushed, and the shirt was stained red, purple and green where I had wiped off my sticky candy hands on past Halloween nights. I had to face the fact that this cowboy had come to the end of his trail.

I went back into the kitchen and shut off the drum CD. I knew what I had to do. When JJ and Cecil arrived at six o'clock, I would greet them at the door, admire their costumes, and wish them well with their trick-or-treating.

Because I didn't really feel like Halloweening this year.

• • •

The torrent of phone calls had slowed to a trickle. That afternoon I did my homework, spent a little time on my latest fantasy character—a crimefighter named Storm Dwayne who could launch tornadoes with a blast from his eyes—and dozed off listening to JJ's Harry Potter CD.

By the time I woke up, evening shadows were slanting through the blinds in my room. I stretched and wandered down the hall. When I passed Chris's room, I was surprised to see that Mom was home. I hadn't heard her come in. I was going to say hello, but the way she was acting made me stop at the doorway.

She was folding a basket of Chris's clean laundry, but she handled every piece of clothing so slowly that it almost looked like she was moving underwater. She carefully smoothed the wrinkles from one sweatshirt, then hugged it as if my brother was still in it.

Finally, so that I wouldn't scare her, I softly said, "Mom?"

She turned and smiled when she saw me. "Hey, honey." She swiped at the corners of her eyes, but I still saw a tear or two.

"You okay?"

"Oh, yeah," she nodded. "I just miss your brother, that's all."

"Me, too."

"I know."

After a long silence, I asked, "Is there anything I can do?"

Mom picked up the laundry basket, and as she

passed me at the door, she patted my cheek. "No. Not a thing."

Not a thing.

I know she probably didn't mean anything by it, but she was right. There *wasn't* anything I could do. After all, what had I done all weekend? I hadn't cooked a meal that anybody had eaten. I hadn't made a Halloween costume. I hadn't visited Chris and, even in my dreams, I stood by like a mailbox while my brother got slammed over and over.

I just felt so *useless*.

Okay, so maybe I am just ten. And not very tall and not very strong. But still, wasn't there something that I could do to make things better? Something to make it so Mom wouldn't feel like crying or . . .

Wait! That was it! I could cheer up Mom. And I knew *just how to do it!*

• • •

My big brother had grown up so quickly that he never wore out any of his clothes, so over the years I inherited all the jerseys and shorts and sweatshirts and running shoes that Chris couldn't fit into anymore. I keep them in the bottom drawer of my dresser, because they actually don't fit me, either. Oh, the size might say "small," but whenever I put on anything from that drawer, I always get swallowed up in the same clothes that Chris used to fill out so well. One time I went downstairs wearing one of Chris's hand-me-downs, and Dad peeked down the back of my shirt and called, "Chris? Chris? Is that you in there? Have you seen your little brother?"

Since then, whenever I'd show up in anything my brother had outgrown, all Dad would have to say was "Remember that time when . . . ?" and Mom would laugh so hard that she'd get hiccups. So when I stood over the drawer filled with Chris's old clothes, I was thinking I could dress up and cheer up Mom before she left. But I had to move fast.

I stripped to my underwear and started digging through the drawer. I slipped on a baseball jersey, but I ripped that off before trying on a pair of running shorts. And then another and another. Clothes I was putting on were getting tangled with clothes I was tearing off. I was hopping around on one leg trying to pull a long-sleeved sweatshirt over my head when Mom called from downstairs.

"Newt, honey? I'm going. There's pizza in the freezer. Or it might be lasagna."

"Mom! Wait till you see this!" I tried to yell, but the sweatshirt muffled my voice.

Frantic, I lunged for my bedroom door, but my feet got twisted in all the clothes I'd been tossing around, and I stumbled backward, falling onto my bed. As I lay there panting, I heard Mom close the garage door. I stared at the ceiling.

"Useless," I groaned.

I stayed there until the doorbell rang.

Was it six o'clock already?

I struggled to my feet and careened into the hallway.

"In a minute!" I shouted.

Halfway down the stairs, I tripped over something I was wearing and tumbled the rest of the way into the entryway. The doorbell rang again. I grabbed the doorknob to pull myself up, and yanked open the front door.

JJ and Cecil took one look at me and gasped. I can't blame them. I was red-faced and sweaty and twisted up in a tornado of Chris's old pants and shirts and shorts.

I took one look at them and gasped, too. Because they looked *amazing*.

JJ was dressed from head to foot in a black gown with a thick silver cord sewn along all the edges. She wore long black gloves, and her hair was twirled around wire pipe cleaners so that it stuck out from her head like rays from a black sun. Her lips were shiny with black gloss, her eyelids were painted with streaks of black and white, and from her ears dangled what looked like silver crystals.

Cecil wore a green velvet jacket crisscrossed with colored ribbons; his green velvet pants were cut short and the bottoms were held in place just below each knee by rubber bands. Long gray socks and green high-top tennis shoes completed the outfit, and he had puffed up his curly black Afro and dusted it with baby talc until it looked like a powdered wig.

"Whoa! You guys!" I sputtered.

"Pretty awesome, huh?" Cecil winked.

JJ smiled as she did a little twirl. "It helps to have four sisters who all know how to sew."

"You wanna know who we are?" Cecil asked.

"Yeah!" I said. "Who are you?"

"Me first!" JJ clapped her hands excitedly. "I am Splendida, the Queen of the Dungeon of Dreams in my favorite, *favorite* saga, *The Crystal Cavern Chronicles*. People think she's an evil witch just because she dresses all in black, but that's only because there are no colors in her world. She's actually the guardian of all the dreams and hopes in the universe, so she's a really good witch. And these," she pointed to her ears, "these are supposed to be the Diamonds of Destiny, but I don't have any diamond earrings. So I made these out of tinfoil and cellophane."

"Awesome," I said, shaking my head in admiration. I turned to Cecil, "And you are . . . ?"

Cecil bowed deeply and made a sound like a trumpet. "Doot-too-doo-DOO! I stand before you tonight as my greatest inspiration, the most excellent musical superfly of the eighteenth century, even though he never wrote a lick for a snare drum or a tom-tom. I am The Wolf—Wolfgang Amadeus Mozart!"

"Mozart!" I cried. "Of course!"

"And my mom let me cut up an old pantsuit of hers,

so don't get any ideas that I run around in velvet all the time, dig?"

"I actually guessed that he was Mozart the moment he walked down the sidewalk," JJ gushed.

I was shaking my head in wonder, stunned by my friends' incredible work, when I realized that they were now staring at me.

"Let me guess," Cecil said. "You're a clothes hamper?"

IN WHICH
I HIDE—
AND FIND MYSELF

I opened my mouth to answer, but nothing came out. Instead, my eyes began to sting and my lower lip started to tremble as everything that had happened in the last forty-eight hours came crashing down on me.

"Dude," Cecil murmured.

"Newt?" JJ asked, gently touching my arm. "Did something happen with Chris?"

I shook my head a little too vigorously. "No, no, he's still asleep," I said, trying to sound cheery. "Catching those z's."

"And you?" Cecil squinted at my outfit. "What's going on here?"

"What? Oh, this?" I tugged at my clothes. "This . . . this was supposed to be a joke. Cuz, see, this stuff's not really mine, but my mom thinks it's hilarious when I put it on, so I . . . I put it on, but before I could show her, she left for the hospital. So ha-ha! Joke's on me!"

I saw Cecil and JJ exchange a look of concern, but I rattled on, speaking faster and faster.

"And there I was, all twisted up in these things and crashing around in my bedroom and rolling down the stairs, and you heard me hit the floor, right? How dumb is that, huh? I mean, how stupid am I to think that I could possibly make any difference . . . and . . . and . . . you know what?" I screeched to a halt. "You guys go ahead without me."

"What?" Cecil cried.

"Why?" asked JJ.

I squeezed my eyes shut and confessed: "Because I didn't make a costume."

Before they could respond, I raced ahead. "I *tried* to think of someone to be. I really did! I concentrated on my inner other, and I made lists of heroes and famous people and stuff, but none of them were me, so instead of being somebody this year, I guess I won't be anybody."

A horrible silence followed my outburst. Finally Cecil tugged at the oversized Windbreaker that was flapping down my back.

"Oh, I don't know," he said. "Doesn't this kind of look like something Superman would wear?"

"It really does," JJ agreed. "And those sweatpants . . . they look like the Hulk's. Sort of."

"I'm *not* gonna be Superman," I groaned. "And I'm sure not the Hulk. Or any of those guys with super-powers who—"

JJ cut me off. "Who says you've got to be any of them?"

"Or any kind of hero that anybody's ever heard of?" Cecil added.

"But what do I say when they ask who I'm supposed to be?" I worried.

"Tell them that you are your own creation," JJ said as she circled me, studying the tangle of fabrics. "The first shining creature of a brand-new breed."

The way the words tumbled out of her mouth made it all sound so important. And possible.

Cecil clapped me on the back. "You got a pair of scissors?"

• • •

First, JJ and Cecil put me in a pair of red sweatpants and tucked them into Chris's old silver track shoes, which were striped with lightning bolts. Next, JJ ripped the sleeves off a gray sweatshirt, cut it down the middle, and with Mom's glue gun she attached the gray fabric to the shoulders of the purple baseball jersey I had on, so that it hung down my back like a puffy cape. And finally, Cecil snipped a single short sleeve off one of Chris's old red T-shirts and tugged it down around my forehead like a sweatband.

They stepped back to inspect their work. JJ shook her head. "It's still lacking something," she said. "There's no *magic* yet."

"I agree," Cecil muttered. "He looks . . . un-magical."

"I look like a gym teacher who got caught in a Laundromat explosion," I moaned.

Just then, JJ snapped her fingers and shouted, "I've got it!" She yanked the sweatband off my forehead, cut two holes in it and pulled it back down past my forehead and over the bridge of my nose.

"A mask!" Cecil exclaimed. "JJ, that's genius!"

"Can you see out the eyeholes?" JJ asked me.

I blinked behind the slits and adjusted the band of fabric.

"I guess," I shrugged.

I swiveled my head around, looking at the ceiling and the floor. But when I turned and saw myself in the front room mirror, I caught my breath.

Because that wasn't me.

Not the Newton Newman who's been staring back at me for ten years. Oh, the clothes were the same as they had been five seconds ago, but the mask had changed everything. The thin strip of fabric that hid my face had turned me into someone I didn't recognize. And—this was even weirder—from inside looking out, I felt protected. Hidden, even.

When JJ cried, "So!" and handed me a candy bag, I took it.

And when Cecil slapped his thigh and declared, "This parade is ready to roll!" I didn't disagree.

8

"Honey! C'mere! You've got to see these kids!"

The jolly, plump man couldn't stop chuckling as we stood on the front porch of the first house we stopped at.

"Oh, my word!" his wife squealed as she joined her husband. She was tall and skinny and wore a wide black witch's hat. In her hands she carried a bowl of Butterfinger bars, which Cecil couldn't take his eyes off of.

"This one," said the man, pointing to Cecil, "he says he's Mozart."

"And I don't doubt it for a second," his wife laughed.

"And this young lady —"

"Don't tell me . . . Splendida!" cried the wife. "Oh,

darling, I've read all the *Crystal Cavern Chronicles*. I'd recognize Splendida anywhere!"

JJ beamed with pride.

Then the husband and wife turned their attention to me. "And who are you supposed to be, little boy?" asked the husband, just the way the neighbor had asked me in my nightmare. The one where I was naked.

I froze.

"Yes," said the wife, looking me over, "who are you, dear?"

Her husband pointed to a spot in the middle of my forehead.

"Are these initials a clue to your identity?"

"What initials?" JJ asked, twisting her head to read from my fabric face mask. "Oh, my. It does say 'C.N.'"

Cecil looked, too. "Who's C.N.?"

I stifled a gasp. In all the rush to build me a costume, I guess that none of us had noticed that the sleeve of my brother's old T-shirt—the sleeve that now circled my head—was stenciled with Chris Newman's initials.

C.N.

"My goodness, yes," said the wife, squinting. "Who *is* C.N.?"

I was tongue-tied. I had never meant to wear Chris's name written across my forehead. And I sure didn't want anybody thinking that I was masquerading *as my brother* on Halloween, not while he was lying in a bed at Appleton General Hospital!

I think that JJ and Cecil sensed my panic, because Cecil suddenly smacked his forehead. "Oh! C.N.! Right . . . okay. Y'see, C.N. stands for . . . uh . . . *Commander*. That's right! Commander . . . uh . . ." I saw him shoot a look to JJ that silently shrieked, *"Help me out here!"*

"Nuclear!" JJ exclaimed with a smile. I could tell she was proud to have pulled such a cool sci-fi word out of thin air.

"Commander Nuclear?" the wife asked.

"Really?" her husband said.

"Yeah," Cecil nodded. "Commander . . ."

"No!" I suddenly snapped.

I surprised everybody—especially myself—when I yelled like that. But I wasn't feeling like myself just then. Behind the mask, I felt like I was somebody . . . oh, I don't know. *New.* Somebody I hadn't met yet.

"You're *not* Commander Nuclear?" Cecil asked, confused.

"Nope."

JJ seemed desperate to find me another name. "Well, sir," she stammered, "are you anyone we've ever heard of?"

"Nope."

"Do you have any powers we should know about?" wondered the wife.

"Nope."

"Okay, then, who *are* you?" her husband asked.

At that moment something—or *somebody*—came

over me. I felt a kind of electric charge race from the top of my head down to my silver lightning-bolt tennis shoes as the answer popped into my brain. I guess I mumbled it so quietly at first that everybody leaned forward and demanded, "What did you say?"

So I pumped up my chest and tossed my cape. I stood with my legs apart and put my fists on my waist. Then with the biggest, bravest smile I had never smiled before, I proudly announced: "You can call me . . . Captain Nobody."

9

IN WHICH
I PRACTICE
MY NEW NAME

Once we got back to the sidewalk, JJ and Cecil exploded with laughter.

"'Captain Nobody?'"

"Where did that come from?"

"You don't like it?" I asked.

"Oh, no, it's *brilliant*!" shouted Cecil. "'Captain
Nobody'—a hero like no other."

"I love it because it sounds mysterious," JJ gushed.
"It's as if you once had another identity, but now some
tragic event has wiped out your memory, and you
are . . . oh!" She suddenly stopped, realizing what she
had said. "Not that what happened to Chris is a *tragic
event*, or anything," she stammered. "I mean, we don't
know whether he's . . ." Her voice trailed off.

"It's okay," I said, patting JJ on the back. "Chris is going to be fine."

Cecil coughed and looked away. He's usually the one who breaks through the awkward moments and gets us back on track, but at that moment, nobody knew what to say.

Without even thinking about what I was doing, I clapped my hands (the way Cecil always does) and shouted "So!" (like JJ).

They both jumped.

"Since my memory has *not* been wiped out," I announced, "I distinctly remember that we were on our way to score some major stash."

And with a mighty whoop, we ran off in search of candy.

• • •

The night was incredible. Our costumes drew gasps and oohs from other trick-or-treaters and from all the people who answered our knocking.

"Astonishing!" they said. "Bravo!"

And we bowed.

As the evening wore on, a strange thing happened. With every house we went to and every doorbell we rang, I felt less and less like Newt. At first, when anyone asked, "And who are you supposed to be?" I would answer, "Captain Nobody," and they would laugh or compliment my style and imagination. But after the first hour or so, I started to answer differently.

"I'm not 'supposed to be' anyone," I corrected them coolly. "I *am* Captain Nobody."

The candy-givers would agree, "Ahh," and nod respectfully. They didn't ask if I had special powers. They didn't demand to see me perform an amazing feat. There was something in the way I announced myself that told people Captain Nobody was the real deal.

Whatever that was.

• • •

We trick-or-treated far later than we ever had in the past. By the end, it was too late to go back to my house and examine our haul, so, after porch lights had been shut off and we had run out of front doors to knock on, we stood on a street corner and took a long, final moment to appreciate each other's costumes.

"We were *not* ignored tonight," Cecil said.

"Yeah," JJ sighed. "I wish we had a camera."

I didn't speak. I felt like any wrong word would pop the bubble of happiness I was floating in at that moment.

"And you—wow! What happened to you tonight?" Cecil asked me.

"Why?"

"You were just so . . . *weird*. But in a supercool way."

I tilted my head. "Oh?"

"Yeah," JJ said. "Every time you spoke, you sounded less like Newt, and more . . . like . . ."

"Like what?"

Her eyes glowed in the light of the streetlamps. "Like Captain Nobody."

• • •

When I got home, Mom's car was in the driveway. But even though the lights were on in the kitchen, she wasn't there. Instead, she had left me a note on the counter, which read:

Dear Newt, did I forget Halloween again??? One of these years I'll remember, and then won't you be shocked? Ha-ha! I hope you had a good time with your friends. I'm going to bed, so I can get up early and trade places with your dad at the hospital. Don't worry about Chris. He's resting comfortably. And don't forget to brush your teeth after eating all that candy. Love, Mom.

There was so much about the evening that was memorable that when I looked down at my Halloween sack, I actually felt silly. *What use could Captain Nobody possibly have for all these gum balls and Pixy Stix? I* pushed my bag of candy down into the kitchen trash and trudged upstairs.

I was a little disappointed, because I hoped I might get home in time to show Mom my costume before I finally took it off. Oh, well.

Still dressed as Captain Nobody, I brushed my teeth. In my bedroom, before I got ready for bed, I turned out the light. Maybe if I undressed in the dark . . . maybe if I didn't see myself without the mask and costume . . . maybe I could make the spell last a little bit longer.

And before I dropped off to sleep, I said it one last time: "I'm not 'supposed to be' anybody. I *am* Captain Nobody."

IN WHICH
I MAKE A WILD
WARDROBE CHOICE

"Newt? I'm going!"

Mom's knock at my bedroom door woke me from a sound sleep. It took me a moment to adjust to my surroundings, because I had just been having a dream, but not the Big Tackle dream. In this one, I—I mean, Captain Nobody—was saving a sinking ship by patching a hole in its side with huge wads of gum that I—or rather, *he*—had been chewing.

"Call my cell phone if you need anything, okay, sweetie?" Mom shouted as she walked away from my door.

"Wait, Mom! How's Chris doing?" I tried to yell, but my voice was still foggy with sleep.

As I heard Mom's car start up and pull out of the driveway, I looked over to my desk chair where I had hung the Captain Nobody outfit the night before. At that moment, in the light of the early morning sun, it looked less like a costume and more like limp hand-me-downs. I climbed out of bed, pulled on the Captain Nobody sweatpants, and went downstairs to eat some breakfast.

I was munching on my cornflakes when I noticed the newspaper Mom had left on the kitchen counter. I couldn't believe it: three days after the Big Game and the whole edition *still* seemed to be about my brother. There were interviews with Chris's teammates, pictures of the crowds in front of the hospital and letters to the editor demanding an investigation into football violence.

There was also a small item on page seven about a bunch of "Fillmore High School troublemakers" who emptied about fifty garbage cans on Reggie Ratner's lawn.

"Fifty cans of garbage," I said out loud. "Wow."

That's when I noticed how quiet it was. Without Chris waking up or my parents racing around, our house felt big and hollow. And sort of sad. So I tried to think cheerful thoughts as I looked around the kitchen: *Chris will be back here in no time, sitting right over there. Mom and Dad will be eating my breakfast very soon, now. We'll be the family we always were. But what if we're not? What if Chris doesn't . . .*

"Stop it!" I cried out. I took a deep breath and shook myself, the way a dog does after a bath.

What could I do to distract myself now?

"Well, don't you have school?" I asked, just the way Mom would have if she'd been there. So I put my dishes in the sink and went upstairs to get dressed.

I was all ready to strip off the red sweatpants and put on jeans, but then I stopped. Just wearing the Captain Nobody pants reminded me of the way I'd felt the night before—strong and assured. Confident that Chris was okay. Certain that Mom wouldn't cry any more. Could I feel that way again?

I slipped on the Captain Nobody shirt with its attached cape, and slid into the silver sneakers.

There! That felt better.

I straightened up and looked at myself in the closet-door mirror.

"What are you doing?" I blurted out to my reflection. "You're still just a scrawny kid."

But then—just for the heck of it—I tugged the mask down over my eyes.

And, what d'you know? All those worries disappeared.

For a long moment, I stared at the boy-who-wasn't-me in the mirror. *Why would I want to be anyone else?* I wondered. Did I really want to trade the specialness of Captain Nobody for the drabness of Newt Newman? Was I really ready to go back to being insignificant and overlooked when I had recently gotten a taste of being so . . . *amazing*?

At that very moment, I caught sight of my bedside clock. Was it really *seven forty-five*?

"I am so dead!" I cried.

Looking for something else to wear, I flung open my closet, only to find that the hangers were almost all empty. Even my dirty clothes basket was gone!

I zoomed downstairs to the laundry room, where I was horrified to discover that, while I was out trick-or-treating, Mom had washed my clothes.

But she had forgotten to dry them.

And the clock on the laundry room wall said *seven fifty*!

"This isn't happening!" I whimpered as I raced back up to my bedroom, where I did the only thing I could do—I tied up the laces of Chris's old track shoes, grabbed my backpack and dashed out of the house.

I sprinted the half mile to school, my silver sneakers stretching out farther and farther as I flew down the sidewalk, almost as if I were growing taller with each stride. As I neared the school, the first bell rang. Everyone on the playground turned and headed into the buildings, so none of the kids really noticed me as I rushed up and filed in behind them.

Once I entered my classroom, though, I got a ton of stares. And snickers.

"What a weirdo!" Basher hooted. "Don't you have a mirror in your house?"

"Halloween's over, loser," sneered Evan McGee,

Basher's buddy. Other kids laughed, too. But then I caught Cecil's eye and he gave me a thumbs-up. JJ looked up from reading. Her mouth dropped open with surprise, but it quickly spread into a smile.

There was a part of my brain that realized how silly I probably appeared to the rest of the world. But, from behind my mask, I looked out and felt . . . okay.

Mrs. Young hurried in and plopped a pile of books and papers on her desk.

"Let's settle down, everyone," she said cheerily. "We have a lot to cover today. We have homework to review, and I want to hear all about your Halloween, and—"

She looked up and saw me.

Every head turned to follow her gaze. Twenty-nine pairs of eyes burned into me, but rather than shrinking in my seat, I sat up straight and tall.

"Uhhhh . . . hello, Newton," she stammered.

"Good morning, Mrs. Young," I answered.

"My. You look . . . uh . . ."

"Like a whack-job," Basher coughed, which made a lot of kids laugh.

"Settle down," Mrs. Young warned as she stepped from behind her desk and looked me up and down. "Let me guess: This was your costume last night, was it?"

"Yes, ma'am," I answered.

"And is there a reason that you've chosen to wear last night's costume to school this morning?"

I shrugged. "It felt right."

"Ah," Mrs. Young nodded.

A few kids snickered, but not as many as before; Mrs. Young's serious tone was having a calming effect on my classmates. "I don't believe I know this . . . character," she said. "Does he have a name?"

I opened my mouth to answer, but Cecil beat me to it.

"Uh, hello?" he exclaimed. "Everybody knows Captain Nobody!"

"Captain Nobody?" Mrs. Young looked startled by the information. Several kids wondered, "Huh?" "Captain Nobody?" "Who's that?"

JJ stood up. "Oh, come on! Don't tell me you don't recognize Captain Nobody. Defender of the little guy? Champion of the downtrodden?"

She was so passionate and convincing that, almost in unison, my classmates grunted, "Oh. Him," and they nodded as if they had known my name all along.

Mrs. Young seemed to be giving the situation some thought. She looked at me with a sympathetic smile and asked, "Newt? How's your brother?"

• • •

"Unacceptable!" Principal Toomey banged his desk. "The boy's obviously toying with us."

I sat outside his office and listened through the half-open door while he and Mrs. Young discussed me. Or, rather, Captain Nobody.

"But I'm sure you heard about what happened to Chris Newman at the Big Game," Mrs. Young said.

"Heard about it? I was there!" Mr. Toomey boomed. "A terrible moment."

"I agree," Mrs. Young said. "I was there, too."

"But what's that got to do with this boy sitting outside my office in a Halloween costume?"

"This 'boy,' Mr. Toomey, is Newton Newman. Chris Newman's younger brother."

"What?" barked Mr. Toomey. "I didn't know Chris Newman *had* a younger brother."

"Well, he does," Mrs. Young replied. "And I can only imagine that this weekend hasn't been an easy one for the Newman family."

"No, I'm sure," Mr. Toomey mumbled. "So what are you saying?"

"I'm only saying that, with his brother in the hospital and both his parents distracted, life at Newton's house may be a little . . . chaotic right now."

"So you think this wacky costume that Newell is wearing—"

"Newton."

"—that Newton is wearing is somehow a result of that chaos?"

"I do. It doesn't worry me that he's wearing that costume. What worries me is his state of mind."

"Why? What's his state of mind?"

"Well," Mrs. Young explained carefully, "he's asking to be called Captain Nobody."

"He *what*?"

I heard Mr. Toomey pick up the phone and call Mr. Brockman, the school counselor. Ten seconds later, Mr. Brockman clomped through the waiting room. He glanced at me as he entered the principal's office and shut the door.

Shortly after that, Mrs. Marcus, the school nurse, hurried in to join them. For about twenty minutes, all I could hear was murmuring, before the door opened and the four adults filed into the waiting room. I stood and faced them.

"We're very sorry about your brother's accident," Mrs. Young said.

"He's going to be okay, Mrs. Young," I assured her.

The adults all exchanged solemn looks.

"Of course he is," Mrs. Marcus nodded.

She shot a look at Mr. Toomey, which seemed to be a cue for him to speak. He wiped the sweat from his forehead and smiled down at me.

"And, I want you to know, young man, Captain Nobody is always welcome in this school."

"Thank you, Mr. Toomey," I said. "Can I go back to class now?"

• • •

"Check it out, check it out!" Cecil whispered excitedly when I set my tray down next to his and JJ's at lunch period.

"What?" I asked.

"Don't look now, but"—JJ giggled—"just look around."

I craned my neck to find that most of the kids in the cafeteria were gawking at our table.

"I said don't look!" hissed JJ.

"But you also said, 'look around,'" I whispered out the side of my mouth.

"Y'see what's happening?" Cecil asked. "Can you feel the electricity?"

"I just see a lot of people who've stopped chewing," I muttered. "You'd think people had never seen old gym clothes before."

"It's not just the clothes." Cecil rapped on the lunch table to make his point. "No! They're diggin' the whole Captain Nobody *vibe*."

"Y'think?"

He and JJ nodded solemnly.

"So, here's what we gotta do," Cecil announced. "From now on, you're gonna be Captain Nobody, and we're gonna be your . . . your . . ." He whipped around to JJ. "What'd you say they call those guys?"

JJ quickly answered, "Sidekicks."

"Sidekicks. Exactly!" Cecil whooped. "So, you're gonna be the one who has adventures, and we're gonna be the ones by your side. *Kickin'*. Like Batman has Robin, y'know? Or Superman has Jimmy Aspirin."

"Olsen," JJ corrected him. "Jimmy Olsen."

"Wait, wait, wait, guys!" I held up both hands. "You're forgetting: I don't have 'adventures.'"

"Not yet!" Cecil said. "But when me and JJ see something suspicious, y'know, and we call you on our cell phones . . ."

"But none of us has a cell phone," JJ interrupted.

"True!" declared Cecil, as if he'd been waiting for that cue. "And that's why we're all going to carry one of these."

From his backpack, Cecil slid a walkie-talkie across the table to me. That's when I began to suspect that maybe the two of them had practiced this little scene in advance.

"I still had these in my locker from a report I did on radio waves," Cecil quickly explained. "I've only got one for me and you right now, but tomorrow, JJ, I'll bring one for you, too."

"And why do I need this?" I asked, inspecting the walkie-talkie.

"So when there's an emergency . . . ," Cecil started.

". . . we can call on you," JJ finished.

"Why would you guys 'call on me'?" I asked.

"In case there's . . . I don't know . . . *danger*?" Cecil suggested.

"He's right," JJ jumped in. "What if somebody needs saving? Or some wrong needs righting or—"

"Stop!" I came very close to shouting. "This is Appleton. Nothing ever happens here. Nothing ever happens to me. I only dressed like this today because . . . because it felt good."

"And it's only gonna feel better," Cecil promised.

JJ looked me in the eyes. "Look what happened, Newt . . . I mean, *Captain*, in just one morning. You heard how Mrs. Young talked to you. You feel what happens when you walk into a room. You see the looks on everybody's faces."

"But what if I wake up tomorrow morning and decide I want to be Newt?"

"Why would you do that?" Cecil was astonished.

"Why wouldn't I?"

"Because," JJ almost wailed, "as long as you're Captain Nobody, and we're by your side, people can't ignore us . . . *ever, ever again*!"

11

IN WHICH
CAPTAIN NOBODY
FACES A FEAR

I never would have expected the changes I saw in my schoolmates. As the day went on, I got the feeling that the theory linking my appearance as Captain Nobody with my brother's accident had made the rounds. By the end of school, the teasing I encountered earlier had turned to curiosity and even sympathy. People who had sneered or stared bug-eyed before lunch began asking, "Howzitgoin'?" as they passed me in the hallways. A few even patted me on my cape and encouraged me to "be strong."

As I walked home that afternoon, amused and puzzled by my day, I remembered that my parents hadn't seen me yet. How would they react? They might have laughed to see me in Chris's old clothes on Halloween night, but what if they freaked out now? Upsetting them was the last thing I wanted to do.

I broke into a run, determined to get back home and change before Mom or Dad got back from the hospital. And I would have made it, too, if Cecil's walkie-talkie hadn't squawked just then.

"This is Cecil Butterworth calling Captain Nobody. Come in. Over," came the scratchy voice from inside my backpack.

For a moment I considered ignoring Cecil, but when he added, *"I'm not foolin' around. Over,"* I laughed and pulled the walkie-talkie from my bag.

"What do you want, Cecil?"

He sounded out of breath. *"When you're finished talking, you're supposed to say, 'over,'"* he said. *"Over."*

I sighed. "Okay. 'Over,' already."

"That's better," he replied. *"Captain Nobody, come quick! Over."*

"What? Why?" There was a long silence until I figured out what he was waiting for. I pressed the "send" button and grumbled, "Over."

"I can't explain, but meet me in three minutes at the corner of Warren and Kander. Over," he said. And before I could say, "What for?" Cecil snapped off his receiver.

I paced back and forth on the sidewalk, caught halfway between my house and the street corner Cecil had named. The way Cecil had shouted *"Captain Nobody, come quick!"* had tweaked my curiosity. So I had a choice: I could go home and change clothes in time to greet my parents, or I could spend just a *little* longer as my inner other.

What would you have done?

• • •

Cecil started waving frantically the moment I turned onto Kander Street. "Captain Nobody! Thank goodness you're here!" He was holding the long, black handle of a low, red wagon.

"What's that for?" I asked as I got nearer. "And what's so important that I had to come quick?"

"I could tell you," Cecil said as he headed down a nearby alley, "but it's easier just to show you."

I followed as he pulled the wagon, bumping and bouncing over the potholed asphalt, past Dumpsters and garbage cans.

"There!" he exclaimed as he pulled to a stop. "Have you ever seen anything so beautiful?"

On top of a Dumpster packed full to the brim with crates and boxes sat a big bass drum. Its shiny metallic blue frame was dented all over and one of its two little kickstand legs was bent at a wonky angle.

"It's pretty banged up," I noted.

"Not where it matters!" Cecil assured me. "Look at that skin—not a tear anywhere."

It was true. From where we stood, the drumhead—the place you hit to make the noise—looked pretty good.

"Even so," I said slowly, "there's a reason someone threw it away."

"So what if it's got a few dings? That doesn't change the sound." Cecil gazed up fondly. "It's the first piece in my very own drum kit."

After a long silence, I finally spoke. "Hey, Cecil? I don't mean to break up your little love affair with the garbage, but why am *I* here?"

"Because! There's no way I could possibly climb up there and bring that thing down alone."

The way the Dumpster loomed over my head, it might as well have been a skyscraper. My fear of heights immediately kicked in as my palms began to sweat.

"You know what?" I suggested. "Why don't *you* climb up there and hand it down to *me*?"

"Well, that's just dumb," Cecil scoffed. "If I slip and drop it, that thing could crush you."

"But if I slip and drop it, then *you'll* be crushed," I pointed out, before adding quietly, "And besides, you know I hate heights."

"That's why this job calls for Captain Nobody. He's fearless!"

Cecil said that last part with such conviction that my heart gave a little kick in my chest. After all, who knew what Captain Nobody was capable of? This discarded drum was Cecil's dream. And there it was . . . just out of reach. How could I *not* help?

I set down my book bag and, wiping my damp palms

on my red sweatpants, I walked to the back of the Dumpster. Slowly and carefully, I climbed the rungs sticking out the side of the big steel box. When I reached the top, I pulled myself over onto the trash heap and stood up.

Big mistake! The instant I saw how high up I was, I dropped to my hands and knees, panting furiously. Fortunately, Cecil was so busy positioning his wagon that he didn't see my panic.

"I'm not 'supposed to be' anybody," I reminded myself in a whisper. "I *am* Captain Nobody."

That calmed me down enough that I managed to crawl over the piles of crumpled boxes, lawn cuttings and plastic garbage bags. When I reached the drum, I tugged it to the front lip of the bin and called down, "Y'ready?"

"Ready!" Cecil shouted. But when I looked over the edge of the Dumpster, I found that he was standing in the bed of his red wagon, reaching up.

"Get out of that thing, Cecil!" I yelled down. "If it rolls, you're going down like Humpty Dumpty."

"Oh. Good thinking." He hopped to the pavement and pushed the wagon to one side. "See? That's why you're Captain Nobody and I'm the sidekick."

It was hard work, but by gripping the drum's battered rim and letting it slide over the side, I was able to slowly ease it down into Cecil's waiting hands.

"Got it?" I asked.

"Got it," Cecil grunted, taking the full weight of his

treasure into his upstretched arms. He staggered for a moment, dropped to one knee, and lowered the drum into his red wagon with a thump. Then he straightened up and, with an open palm, he thwacked the drum skin.

Boom!

"Wow . . . wow . . . wow," Cecil repeated over and over.

I guess it had all been worth it.

With great care, I crawled back to the rear of the Dumpster and swung a leg over the edge. My foot searched around until it found the first rung, and then I clambered down backward.

I was feeling pretty pumped up from my first "adventure." At least until a gnarled hand suddenly shot out from a stack of cardboard boxes piled against the wall and grabbed me by the ankle!

I screamed like a cheerleader in a horror film.

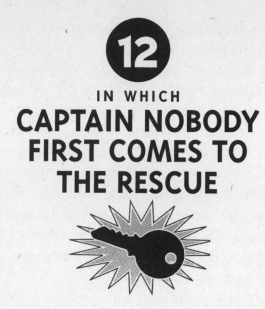

12

IN WHICH
CAPTAIN NOBODY
FIRST COMES TO
THE RESCUE

"What's goin' on, man?" Cecil hollered as he dashed around the corner of the Dumpster.

The hand belonged to an old, gray-whiskered man slumped on the pavement. When Cecil saw the guy, he shouted, "Hey! You! Get offa him, mister!"

The man flinched at the sound of Cecil's voice. He let go of me, and then he shook his head and rubbed his red eyes as if he were just waking up. My first thought was that this guy was drunk and had stumbled into the alley to sleep. But once I got over the shock of being grabbed, I saw that he was sort of nicely dressed.

And that's when I realized that I knew him.

"Mr. Clay?"

The man looked up at me and blinked. "Tuesday. It's Tuesday," he said.

"You know this guy?" Cecil asked.

"Mr. Clay's a locksmith," I explained.

I should have said, Mr. Clay *was* a locksmith. Over the years, Mom would sometimes arrive at a house she was trying to sell only to discover that she had forgotten—or lost—the keys. That's when she'd call Mr. Clay. He'd zip right over and pick the locks or re-key the doorknobs, and then he'd cut extra keys with the machine he had in the back of his little cherry red van. Mom had used him for as long as I could remember, but about a year ago, I overheard her tell Dad, "I'm afraid that sweet Mr. Clay is beginning to drop the ball." She hasn't called him since.

Mr. Clay looked up with wide, watery eyes and extended a closed fist to me.

"Watch it!" Cecil warned. "The guy's probably a wino."

"Mr. Clay's not a wino," I said. "But I think he's got that thing older people get . . . where their mind gets fuzzy?"

"Oh, yeah," Cecil said. He gave Mr. Clay a sympathetic look. "My Grandma Butterworth got that. It's no fun."

I reached my hand out to his. Mr. Clay dropped an empty plastic medicine bottle into my palm.

"Oh, I get it. He's out of medicine," I explained to Cecil. "Is that what happened, Mr. Clay? Did you go for a walk and get lost?"

He stared at me, confused and hesitant. "Do I know you?"

I knelt down and took him by the arm.

"Mr. Clay, my name is Captain Nobody," I said, helping him to his feet, "and I'm here to take you home."

• • •

I held Mr. Clay's hand and walked him the six blocks to his house. I knew where he lived, because when he wasn't off doing a job, his cherry red van was always parked in front. Cecil followed us, hauling his drum in the wagon. None of us said anything until we turned onto Mr. Clay's block.

"I know this street," he smiled weakly.

"I bet you do," I assured him.

Cecil waited on the sidewalk as I led Mr. Clay up on his front porch. I was about to ring the doorbell when he put out his hand to stop my finger.

"Mrs. Clay will be worried," he said with an embarrassed wince.

I nodded and left him there on the porch so he could ring the bell himself.

By the time I'd run down the driveway and joined Cecil at the curb, the front door had opened and a woman's voice cried, "There you are! I was worried sick!"

Over a low hedge, Cecil and I watched as a little lady with gray hair in a flowered dress—Mrs. Clay, I guessed—hugged Mr. Clay with all her might.

"How did you get here?" we heard her ask in a voice choked with emotion.

"Captain Nobody walked me home," said Mr. Clay.

"Oh. Captain Nobody, huh?" Mrs. Clay chuckled as she scanned the empty porch and wiped tears from her face. "I hope you thanked him." She gently led Mr. Clay into the house and closed the door.

Cecil and I exchanged a smile.

"You saved that man," Cecil said.

"Oh, c'mon," I scoffed. "I walked an old friend home."

He held up a hand, and I high-fived him. Then we rolled his precious bass drum over to his house, thumping it as we went.

13

IN WHICH
DAD MEETS
CAPTAIN NOBODY

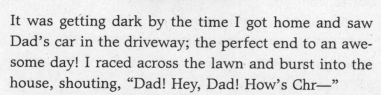

It was getting dark by the time I got home and saw Dad's car in the driveway; the perfect end to an awesome day! I raced across the lawn and burst into the house, shouting, "Dad! Hey, Dad! How's Chr—"

I screeched to a halt in the kitchen doorway when I saw that Dad was on his cell. He looked me up and down, and said into his phone, "Listen, let me call you back" before folding it shut.

That's when it hit me that Dad was meeting Captain Nobody for the first time.

All thoughts of Chris flew from my head. In the awkward silence that followed, I gulped and shifted from one foot to the other, more nervous and uncomfortable than I had been in the last twenty-four hours. If Mom had been the first to see me dressed the way I was, I'm pretty sure that she'd have been amused, but I couldn't figure out whether Dad was angry or concerned.

Finally he shook his head and said, "We are so sorry, Newt."

"Sorry? For what?"

"For neglecting you." I started to speak, but Dad put his hand up. "No, it's true. We—your mother and I—we've been very, very distracted lately. Then today we started getting calls at the hospital. First it was your principal, then Mrs. Young, then your guidance counselor, and, my gosh, our cell phones were going all day. And we think we owe you an apology, because we . . ." He gave a big sigh. "We just never stopped to notice what you've been going through."

"What am I going through?"

"This!" He waved his hand at my clothes. "The folks at school seem to think that you're so upset about your brother's situation—"

"I never told them that!" I blurted.

"Well, they're smart people. They figure these things out. And they're very concerned—and so are your mom and I—that Chris's accident has disturbed you so much that you seem to have—how'd they put it?—that you seem to have 'lost touch with reality.'"

"I what?" I almost laughed. "They think I'm crazy?"

"Nobody used that word."

"Do *you* think I'm crazy?"

"Well, you wore your Halloween costume to school."

"Yeah, but . . . ," I started to say.

"And they're your brother's clothes."

"He gave them to me, so they're technically mine," I insisted. "And besides, I feel really super *amazing* in them. It's like magic, Dad."

"Clothes do not have magical powers, Newt."

"Really? What about your 'lucky hat' that you wear to all of Chris's games?"

"That's not exactly the same thing—"

"And Mom? When she's close to selling a house, she puts on those green shoes she calls her 'seal-the-deal-heels'?"

"All right, all right, I get it," Dad stammered. "But, still . . . you told people your name is 'Captain Nobody.'"

"Pretty cool, huh? It sort of came to me."

"It *'came'* to you?" Dad looked worried. "This Captain Nobody, what should I know about him? Is he going to try to fly or stop a bullet with his teeth?"

I sighed. "Dad, I haven't lost my mind."

"You're sure?"

"Behind the mask, I'm still me."

That seemed to console him. "Okay, then let me ask you: When do you think you'll . . . stop?"

"Stop?"

"Stop being Captain Nobody."

If Dad had asked me that question two hours before—before I helped Cecil rescue his bass drum and before I saw the light go on in Mr. Clay's eyes—I probably would have had a different answer.

"I'm not sure," I shrugged, and then I did something I don't remember ever having done in my lifetime: I reached up and patted my dad on the shoulder. "But you'll be the first to know," I assured him.

Dad smiled. He seemed relieved to end that conversation. His pager beeped, but he punched the button that switches it off and turned his attention back to me.

"So, are your teachers right?" he asked. "Are you thinking about your brother a lot?"

I felt like I'd been poked in the heart.

"Oh, yeah," I said quietly. "A lot."

• • •

We sat at the kitchen counter and ate sloppy joes that I made from a can. Dad told me how Chris's doctors were "baffled," but they were continuing to "feel optimistic." He talked about the machines Chris was hooked up to and the tests they were running, and how there were so many balloons and flowers in my brother's room that the nurses started to distribute them around the hospital.

Then Dad took a picture of me with his cell phone and sent it to Mom.

Suddenly, in the middle of our great conversation, the walkie-talkie in my backpack squealed.

"What's that?" Dad asked.

I jumped off my chair and grabbed my bag. "Sorry! Cecil's trying out this new gadget on me," I said. "I'll take it in the dining room."

Once I was out of earshot, I pulled out the receiver in time to hear: *"This is Cecil Butterworth calling Captain Nobody. Come in, Captain Nobody. Over."*

I pushed the "talk" button. "What is it now, Cecil?" I groaned before I added, "Over."

"We need you, Captain Nobody! My uncle wants to move a freezer out of his basement, and I told him I know just the guy to call. Over."

I stared in disbelief at the walkie-talkie in my hand before I squeezed the "talk" button again. I made hissing and crackling noises, "kshhrkkkkpppfffsshhhh . . ."—sprinkled with fragments of words—". . . can't hear you . . . pssshhhh . . . losing battery pow . . . bbbbblljjjkkkshhhh." Then, just before switching off the walkie-talkie once and for all, I said very clearly, "Over."

• • •

I finished my homework and was getting ready for bed when Dad stuck his head into my room.

"Your mom got the picture of Captain Nobody. She

says she hasn't stopped laughing, and she's showing everybody in the hospital."

"Really?" My smile was about two feet wide. It seemed like a good moment to ask the question I had been wanting to ask all evening.

"Dad? When can I come visit Chris?"

Dad sat on the edge of my bed and patted a place for me to sit beside him.

"Right now, kiddo, Chris's doctors still have tests they want to run. They have specialists they want to consult. Until then, they're saying, 'No visitors.' As a matter of fact, Chris's coach dropped by, and his teammates keep showing up. But nobody gets in." Dad put an arm around my shoulder. "So, can you give us another day or two before you come by?"

I squeezed my lips together and nodded.

"Sure."

"But," Dad said brightly, "just because you can't visit doesn't mean you can't *see* your brother."

"What do you mean?"

"Well, visiting hours are over for the night," he said, pulling his cell phone out of its holster on his belt, "but look what your mother took for you."

He flipped open his phone, pushed a button, and there, on the tiny screen, was a short, wobbly video of Chris lying in his hospital bed. He looked pretty much the same as when I go to wake him in the morning, except that bundles of wires and tubes snaked out from under his hospital gown and connected him to a bunch of machines with green blips rolling across their screens. Dad explained what every machine was for. Since the little movie lasted only about ten seconds, we played it four more times.

When we were done, my eyes stung and I couldn't think of anything to say. After I closed the phone and handed it back to Dad, he kissed the top of my head. "When the doctors say it's okay, you'll be the first one through the door."

"Thanks," I whispered.

"And now I've got a question," he said as he stood. "Do you go to sleep dressed like that?"

"Dad." I rolled my eyes. "Of course not. Even Captain Nobody needs to rest once in a while."

"And does Captain Nobody ever give his dad a good-night hug?"

I wrapped my arms around him and squeezed real hard. "Tell me if I'm crushing you."

Dad laughed for the first time all night.

● ● ●

I dropped off to sleep and dreamed about the Big Tackle again, only this time, I came to my brother's rescue. Just as Chris was diving over the goal line with both teams stampeding behind him, I raced into the end zone dressed as Captain Nobody, held up both hands and shouted, "Ollie ollie oxen *STOP!*" All twenty-one players froze, some of them in midair.

Once Chris had a chance to walk off the field and was safe, I snapped my fingers, and they all dropped in a heap on the ground. Then I yelled, "Pizza for everyone!" About a thousand pizzas got delivered, and everybody in the stadium got a slice.

I don't really understand that last part.

IN WHICH
CERTAIN THREATS
ARE MADE

It's kind of amazing how quickly people can get used to new ideas. The next day at school, you'd have thought I'd been Captain Nobody since kindergarten. I still got a few stares in the hallways, but nobody made fun of me on the playground. When I raised my hand in class, Mrs. Young called on me by saying, "Yes, Captain Nobody?" And nobody snickered.

At noon, on the playground, I came up behind Cecil as he was explaining to JJ how to operate her walkie-talkie.

"You push this button here, you talk into here, and all you have to say is 'Come quick, Captain Nobody!'"

"Wait a minute!" I interrupted. "What are you calling me for now?"

"It's just in case," Cecil explained.

"I'll only call if it's a real, true emergency," JJ said. "I swear."

"If it's a real, true emergency," I said, "you'd better call 911."

Cecil scowled. *"Anybody* can do that." He held up his walkie-talkie. "The three of us have our own, highly specialized communication network. Speaking of which, what's up with yours, Captain?"

I pulled the unit out of my backpack. "Nothing. Why?"

"Last night when I called? It sounded like you were at the bottom of the ocean."

"I don't know." I shrugged innocently. "This morning I turned it on, and it's good to go."

"Great!" he declared. "So, now we gotta check that we're on the same channel." He pointed to two corners of the school yard. "Let's spread out and run a test."

I leaned over to tell JJ, "And be sure to say 'over' when you're done talking, otherwise Cecil gets very upset."

JJ laughed, but Cecil just smacked me on the shoulder. "Get out there!" he ordered.

JJ went to one end of the playground, and I headed to the other, where a football game was in progress.

My walkie-talkie crackled. *"Cecil, can you hear me?"* It was JJ, who quickly added, *"Over."*

"I read you loud and clear," Cecil answered. *"And Captain Nobody? Are you hearing this? Over."*

I pressed the button and was about to respond when suddenly a football *boinked!* me on the back of the head. I dropped to one knee.

"Ow!" I complained, rubbing my scalp.

"What's the matter? Aren't you supposed to be tougher than steel?"

I looked up. A hulking seventh-grader glowered down at me. Under one massive arm he held the football that had just bounced off my skull. Behind him, a posse of his classmates stood, arms crossed.

My heart was pounding as I got up, but I looked this guy straight in the eye and asked, "Who wants to know?"

"Ricky Ratner. Name ring a bell . . . Newman?"

Startled, I blurted out, "Are you related to *Reggie* Ratner? Over at Merrimac High?"

"Reggie's my cousin."

Although this guy had just beaned me with a ball and his cousin had supposedly knocked out my brother, I couldn't help but gasp, "Man! Your cousin is one awesome defensive end! He played against my brother's team on Frid—"

"Yeah. Friday," Ricky Ratner said bitterly. "And you know what's been happenin' ever since?"

I gulped. "I've heard."

He put his face right up to mine. "What you didn't

hear is that my cousin Reggie had nothing to do with punchin' out your brother's lights."

"I never said he did."

"But everybody else at Fillmore High School thinks he did. So, here's what I want you to do," Ricky said, poking my chest with a thick finger. "I want you to call off your brother's friends and all those stupid football players who keep hasslin' my cousin, because if you don't . . ."

From behind him, Cecil shouted, "Yo!"

Ricky stop jabbing me and turned to face Cecil.

"Yeah, you." Cecil tried to sound tough. "Can I help you?"

Cecil and JJ stood side by side, tiny and tall. Ricky looked them over and cackled. "Don't make me laugh."

"He just did," JJ said.

Ricky sneered. "Just did *what*?"

"Made you laugh," JJ explained. "See, you said, 'Don't make me laugh,' but by that time, you were already laughing, so—"

"How 'bout you shut up?" Ricky barked.

"Hey!" Cecil snapped. "If you got a problem with Captain Nobody, you got a problem with us."

"Oh, I'm scared now!" Ricky scoffed. "I got a problem with *you*?"

Cecil started to respond when, from behind him, came a new voice.

"And us."

We looked up. Behind Cecil and JJ, Basher and Evan McGee and all the rest of the fourth-grade boys—my classmates!—were lined up with *their* arms crossed the way the seventh-graders' were. And even though my classmates were younger and smaller, there were a lot more of them. Together they somehow managed to appear threatening.

Cecil looked to me and raised a single eyebrow, as if to say, "How cool is this?"

Everything was suddenly quiet. All over the school yard, kids from other grades had stopped playing and were watching the showdown. Then—all the way across the field—I saw Mr. Toomey step out of the school building, look in our direction, and fold *his* arms.

Ricky Ratner saw him, too. In the next moment, he seemed to deflate.

"Remember what I said," he hissed at me. "You tell your brother's friends to back off my cousin. Or else."

After a final poke, he turned and blended back into his crowd. Within a split second, the wall of my fourth-grade classmates had dissolved and life on the playground had returned to normal.

I looked at JJ and Cecil and exhaled.

"What was that?" I asked, baffled.

"It's happening just like we said it would," JJ smiled broadly.

"*What's* happening?"

Cecil threw his arms open wide. "It's the power of Captain Nobody," he crowed. "We're finally getting *noticed!*"

• • •

After school, I carefully scoped out the school yard, worried that Ricky Ratner and the rest of the seventh grade would be lying in wait for me. I didn't see any signs of danger, but just to be sure, I slipped out through the faculty parking lot and headed home. I guess my nerves were still a little raw from my earlier confrontation, or else I wouldn't have jumped about two feet off the pavement when, from out of my backpack, I heard: *"Captain Nobody? It's JJ! Do you read me? Over!"*

"Now what?" I groaned to myself.

"Captain Nobody, I need your help!" JJ yelled. *"Please come in. Or answer. Or whatever you're supposed to say. Over."* After a pause, she continued. *"I'm serious. Captain Nobody, I wouldn't be calling if this wasn't really, really important, and since this is the first time I'm asking for anyth—"*

I couldn't stand it! I ripped the walkie-talkie from my backpack and hit the button. "Captain Nobody speaking! Over."

"Oh, thank goodness you're there! This is an emergency, I'm not kidding. Meet me immediately in front of Sullivan's Jewelry Store on Duncan Street. Over."

"Actually, JJ," I said, "I'm supposed to go right home today. Sorry. Over."

"But you don't understand." JJ was whining now. *"The most horrible thing has happened, and, oh, my god. . . . Nooooo!"* JJ suddenly screamed.

I gasped as my walkie-talkie went dead. I shook it and punched the buttons, yelling, "JJ! JJ? Do you read me? Come in, JJ! Over," but there was no longer any signal.

I had no choice. I sprinted off toward Sullivan's Jewelry Store, terrified of what I would find when I got there.

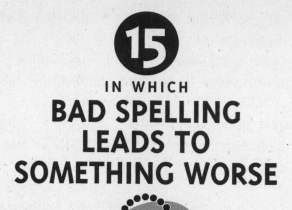

15

IN WHICH
BAD SPELLING
LEADS TO
SOMETHING WORSE

I zigzagged through backyards and alleys to get to Duncan Street as fast as my silver sneakers would carry me. There I found JJ standing at the curb in front of Sullivan's Jewelry Store, her face buried in her hands.

"JJ!" I panted as I raced to her side. "What's wrong?"

"Oh, I don't even know where to start," she moaned.

"Start at the beginning," I suggested, trying to sound calm in the middle of what was surely a ghastly tragedy.

She shook back her hair and cleared her throat. "Okay. It all began with that." She pointed to Sullivan's front window, where rows of sparkling rings and racks of colorful necklaces were on display.

"What am I looking at?"

"The sign!" she wailed. "That horrible, handwritten sign."

It read:

ASK ABOUT OUR 24 CARROT GOLD!

"That's not how you spell 'karat,'" I said automatically.

"Exactly!" JJ practically shrieked through clenched teeth. "And don't even get me started about the one over there."

She gestured to another card:

EVERY NECKLESS ON SALE.

"Ouch," I winced.

"Right?" JJ shouted. "I can't tell you how many times I've gone in there and tried to talk to Mr. and Mrs. Sullivan, but do they listen? Do they correct these crimes against the language? No! They only say, 'Thank you and good-bye, little girl.'"

I was starting to get annoyed. "And you're upset because of a few spelling mista—"

"Oh, if only that were all!" she cut me off. "Even as I stood here, talking to you on Cecil's walkie-talkie,

look what Mr. Sullivan just slipped in, not five minutes ago!"

A piece of white cardboard leaning against the opposite display window proclaimed

ALL EARRING'S HALF OFF!!!

"So?" I asked in disbelief. "He misplaced an apostrophe, and you screamed?"

"Oh, tell me you're not horrified!" JJ exploded.

"I'm not," I shrugged.

"But it's so wrong! If I have to pass by one more day
and see these . . . these *massacres* of grammar and
spelling, I'm going to have to find another way to walk
to school."

I was speechless until JJ finally asked, "So will you
talk to them?"

"Me?" I cried. "Why me?"

JJ threw her arms up. "You're Captain Nobody! 'Defender of the little guy, champion of the downtrodden.' Remember?"

"Why would they even listen to me, JJ?"

"Because," she sighed. "People notice you."

At that moment, JJ—who usually comes off as being
so smart and confident—suddenly seemed so . . . not
those things. It's funny how much clearer the world
looks from behind a mask.

"Hold my book bag," I said.

• • •

A door chime announced my entrance into the store. The square shop was bordered by glass counters, and four or five more display cases stood around in the middle of the floor. I had been there only once, years before, when Dad had a watchband replaced, but it didn't look as if anything had changed. The counters were still cluttered with mirrors and spinning racks of gold chains and silver bangles. Music played softly from speakers in the ceiling.

At the far end of one aisle, Mr. and Mrs. Sullivan— gray-haired and proper—stood side by side behind a counter, waiting on the only customer in the store. They looked up when I entered, and their mouths fell open. I guess they didn't get many masked shoppers wearing red sweatpants and silver shoes. The customer, however, peered at me over his sunglasses, and he didn't even blink. He was unshaven, and he wore a zip-up sweatshirt and a baseball cap pulled low over his face.

Once Mr. Sullivan got over the initial shock, he asked, in a thick Irish accent, "And how can I be helpin' you, little . . . person?"

"I . . . I . . . I can wait," I stammered. "Or better yet, I'll come back when you're not so busy."

I spun on my heels and would have marched out, but Mrs. Sullivan suddenly cried, "No, please!"

I turned back and looked at Mrs. Sullivan, really

looked at her. Which was something new. When I'm around adults I usually spend most of the time staring at the ground under my feet. But the day before I had looked Mr. Clay in the eye as we stood on his front porch, and now I was meeting Mrs. Sullivan's look with a steady gaze of my own.

"Every customer is important to us," she said with a tight smile, speaking with the same Irish accent her husband had. "What is it that you'll be needing?"

I got a strong feeling that it was important to her that I stay. So I stepped forward. "It's kind of stupid," I began, pointing over my shoulder, "but it's about your signs."

"Me signs?" Mr. Sullivan sniffed.

"The signs in the window? There's something wrong with a few of them," I explained, moving closer. "Little things. Spelling things. Punctuation stuff."

As I neared the countertop I noticed all the merchandise that the Sullivans had laid out for their customer's approval: bracelets and watches and diamond rings, all glinting under the fluorescent lights.

"Oh, I'm sorry," I blurted. "I didn't mean to interrupt a sale."

"Then don't!" the customer growled at the same time that Mrs. Sullivan exclaimed, "Don't be silly!"

"Okay, it's only three things." I spoke very quickly. "First, 'twenty-four karat' is spelled K-A-R-A-T. The way you've got it now, it's a vegetable."

The customer sighed with annoyance, so I sped up even more.

"Second, the way you wrote 'necklace' out there, it's like 'neck-*less*,' which means 'without a neck,' and without a neck, you'd have no place to hang a necklace, so you might want to take a look at that, okay?"

While I was talking, Mr. and Mrs. Sullivan's eyes kept darting between me and the merchandise and their customer. The customer was twitching with irritation, his right hand poking forward in his sweatshirt pocket as if he were holding on to something in there and pointing it at Mr. and Mrs. Sulliv—

Holy moly! I screamed inside my head. *Has he got a gun?*

I looked from the customer's pocket to Mr. and Mrs. Sullivan, whose eyes were now huge. My mouth was suddenly bone-dry.

"And what else?" Mrs. Sullivan's question snapped me back to reality.

"Huh?" I blinked.

"What else is wrong with our signs?" Mrs. Sullivan asked. "This is very helpful."

"Very helpful!" Mr. Sullivan repeated. "Matter of fact, I should be writin' down these suggestions. Now, where's me pen?"

He turned to a desk behind him.

"Stop right there!" shouted the customer. But it was too late.

Mr. Sullivan's hand slipped under the desktop and pressed a hidden button. A shrill alarm suddenly split the air.

In the next second, everybody exploded into action.

Mrs. Sullivan ducked behind the display case as Mr. Sullivan shouted into a phone, "Hello? POLICE?" The customer—oh, all right—the *thief* swept an arm across the countertop and hugged a pile of jewelry against his chest. He spun around, and *wham!* ran smack dab into me.

We tumbled to the floor as diamonds and watches spilled in every direction. The guy grabbed my collar and barked, "Breathe one word about this, I will hunt you down and I *will* hurt you!" Then he scrambled to his feet and raced out.

I jumped up, trying not to step on all the gems and necklaces underfoot. The alarm was shrieking, Mrs. Sullivan was sobbing, and Mr. Sullivan was ranting into the phone. It wasn't a good time, I realized, to explain about the unnecessary apostrophe in "earring's."

So I left.

•••

"What's going on?" JJ yelled above the wail of the alarm as I rocketed past her.

"There was a robber in the store!" I called over my shoulder.

JJ yelled after me, "Was that the guy who just ran out?"

I whirled around. "Where'd he go?"

"I don't know," she shrugged. "The alarm distracted me."

In the distance, we could hear police sirens. I grabbed JJ's hand and dragged her behind me. "We've got to get out of here!"

"But shouldn't you stay and talk to the police?" she cried.

I reached up and took JJ by the shoulders. "That robber said he would hunt me down and hurt me if I tell anybody *anything*."

"But you just told me," JJ said.

I gulped. "Then we're both in danger!" I wailed, pulling her along.

She shook loose of my hand. "But you're a witness," she insisted. "You have a responsibility!"

"And the bad guy has a gun!" I shouted.

We both ran.

16

IN WHICH
I DON'T APPEAR ON THE FIVE O'CLOCK NEWS

"Captain Nobody!" Mom exclaimed when I finally got home late that afternoon. She kissed my forehead. "You're even more handsome than your picture."

"Hey, Mom," I said, hoping that she wouldn't hear how furiously my heart was beating. "How's Chris?"

"Well, his color's coming back," she said brightly between sorting the mail and stirring a pot of chili on the stove. "He'd been looking sort of gray there for a few days, but today . . . bingo! The doctors are so pleased— all nine of them. He has nine doctors, imagine that. Matter of fact, there's a specialist coming in to see him this afternoon. All the way from Minnesota!"

Something was wrong. The more upset Mom gets, the faster she talks, and she was chittering away like a windup toy.

"What's the specialist coming for?" I just managed to ask before the phone rang. Mom held up a hold-that-thought finger before she answered. She listened for a moment and then covered the mouthpiece.

"It's . . . it's about one of my houses," she said nervously, though it clearly wasn't. "Have a cookie. Have two," she called out as she stretched the phone cord down the hall and into her office.

I poured myself a glass of milk and switched on the little TV in the breakfast nook. Across the top of the screen a banner read: "Daring Daylight Heist." The picture came into focus, and my eyes nearly popped out of my head when I saw that our local TV reporter was standing in front of *Sullivan's Jewelry Store*!

". . . when, without warning, the robber demanded thousands of dollars in jewels and threatened the owners with a gun," she was saying. "I asked the store's owners to tell us how they reacted at that moment."

Mr. and Mrs. Sullivan appeared on-screen, standing behind the counter where I last saw them.

"When the man first said he had a gun," Mrs. Sullivan said in her lilting Irish way, "I'm afraid I just froze in me shoes."

"We both did, darlin'." Mr. Sullivan patted his wife's hand. "We'd probably still be standin' here like two big, dumb rocks if it weren't for the little guy who wandered in."

I spit milk from my mouth. *"The little guy?"*

"Yes, they're calling him 'the little guy,'" the reporter

seemed to answer me. "As you can see from this surveillance video"—they cut to a silent black-and-white video of the robbery—"the Sullivans and their assailant are apparently reacting to the entrance of another person into the store . . ."

On the screen you could see the three of them turning to look at—hey! *Where was I?*

". . . but there are no pictures of the Sullivans' savior."

"Yeah, the surveillance cameras are aimed so they only pick up normal-sized people," a gruff policeman was explaining to the reporter. "Otherwise, the display cases block the view of anything, uh . . . subnormal. We suspect that the person the Sullivans saw was a midget."

"A midget?" I winced.

"It's clear that somebody interrupted this crime in progress," the reporter was finishing up, "and, quite possibly, saved a couple of lives in the process. Exactly who that was will remain a mystery, although the Sullivans have a theory about their hero."

"We Irish have our legends about the wee folk who do good deeds," Mr. Sullivan explained. "Leprechauns, we call them."

"This one wasn't dressed in green," Mrs. Sullivan laughed, "but he brought us luck, I'll tell you that."

"Now I'm a leprechaun," I groaned, before Mom suddenly appeared behind me. "Phone's for you! It's JJ."

Flustered, I took the receiver and answered, "What's up?"

"Are you watching the news?" JJ screamed.

I hurried into the living room so Mom wouldn't hear. "I just saw," I whispered.

"How amazing is *that*?" JJ squealed. "It's your third day as Captain Nobody, and you're already on the five o'clock news!"

"Not if you look closely," I said.

"Well, okay, they didn't get a shot of you, but we know who saved the day, don't we?"

"Yeah. It was a 'little guy' who's either a 'midget' or maybe a 'leprechaun.' I'm branded for life."

"Nobody's going to call you that once they learn what you did!"

"JJ, we can't talk about this. To *anyone*," I stressed.

"Why not?" she whimpered. "This is the most exciting thing that's happened to anyone I know since my sister Theresa got stuck in the elevators at the mall for eleven hours and she had to pee in a cup."

"Yeah, that was pretty exciting," I remembered. "But the last thing I want to do right now is to put my family in the middle of another crisis."

"But what if the robber didn't have a gun?" she persisted. "And what if he didn't threaten to hunt you down and hurt you?"

"But he did."

"Okay, okay, we won't tell anyone," she mumbled.

Then she perked up. "Except for Cecil! Who gets to tell Cecil?"

• • •

Mom and I ate dinner together that night. Even though it was obvious that something was bothering her, she never brought it up. So finally I did.

"Is something going on with Chris?" I asked.

"No," she answered too quickly. "No. Just the usual."

She smiled cheerfully, but her eyes were shiny wet. "But tell me about your day, Captain Nobody. Anything happen?"

"Nope," I lied. "Not a thing." I stood and began to clear our plates.

She started to rise. "Oh, I can do that."

I laid a hand on her shoulder and sat her down. "Relax, Mom. I got this." I carried the dishes into the kitchen. A few minutes later, as I washed them at the sink, I heard Mom sniffling and blowing her nose into a napkin.

I guess we both had our secrets.

• • •

Before I went to bed that night, I took off my Captain Nobody costume and folded it carefully. I looked down at the clothes, thinking back to all that had happened in the short time I had been wearing them, and wondering if it was time to stop. After all, if I'd been dressed as Newt today, I would never have listened to JJ and agreed to talk to the Sullivans. So I would never have walked in on a crime in progress, and I wouldn't have to live in fear for the rest of my life.

On the other hand, I probably wouldn't have saved the Sullivans from being robbed.

Or gotten the chance to help Mr. Clay the day before.

So . . . to *be* Captain Nobody or *not* to be. That was my question.

That night I dreamed that Chris was sitting on the edge of my bed, flipping through one of my schoolbooks, just like the time I got the mumps and had to miss school for two weeks. Chris arranged with my teacher to bring my homework home, and night after night he sat with me and explained the multiplication table and how to write a capital *B* in script.

"Whoa, Chris! How are you?" I asked excitedly, sitting up and wrapping my arms around him.

"Mom says my color's returning," he laughed. "And how about you? How you doin', Captain?"

When I heard him use my new name, I puffed up with pride, but before I could answer his question, Chris faded from view, and I was left hugging thin air.

● ● ●

I woke to an empty house and ate breakfast standing up at the kitchen counter. I unfolded the *Appleton Sentinel* and couldn't believe my eyes! There, on the front page, was the headline: "Appleton Police Arrest Armed and Dangerous Jewel Thief."

Apparently, the robber was still wearing the same baseball cap and sweatshirt when he went into a McDonald's near the Sullivans' store. As he was ordering a Big Mac and a Coke, the five o'clock news came up on an in-store TV. Immediately, a lady pointed and screamed, "That's the guy!" People started pelting the thief with burgers and french fries and milk shakes, and when he ran for the door, he slipped on all the wet food at his feet. The thief thrashed around on the sticky floor until a very brave—and very heavy—man sat on him and stayed there until the cops arrived.

My *whoop!* of joy was so loud that our neighbors' dogs started barking. I jumped off my stool and did a little victory dance around the kitchen, until I spied a ripped newspaper page sticking out of the trash bin. Why was Mom throwing out the paper before I'd had a chance to read it? The headline on that discarded page caught my eye: "Medical Expert Estimates Newman's Okay for Six Days."

I snatched up the torn page and began to read how the brain specialist from Minnesota Mom had told me about had advised my parents and Chris's doctors that they should have "no significant concern" about Chris's condition . . . "unless it persists for more than six days."

Six days? It was now Wednesday. Chris had been tackled on Friday. I counted: Saturday, Sunday, Monday, Tuesday, Wednesday . . . Tomorrow would be six days. He *had* to wake up tomorrow, or else . . . or else *what*?

"What happens after six days?" I shouted at the newspaper in my shaking hands. I read the article three more times, but I still couldn't find an answer. And then a sudden thought stopped me cold: Mom and Dad must be more worried than they had been letting on. I bet that's why Mom had been fighting back tears the night before, and that's why she had torn the article out of the morning paper.

"Oh, my gosh!" I gasped when I made the biggest realization of all: Mom and Dad had been keeping me away from the hospital *to protect me!*

A bunch of different feelings collided in my chest. I felt foolish for whining all week about wanting to visit Chris. Plus, I felt stupid for not figuring things out sooner. And, worst of all, I felt really, really scared.

Back in my bedroom, my choice of clothes was an easy one. Now, more than ever, I needed the protection of Captain Nobody.

17

IN WHICH
I CHEAT DEATH

By the time I got to school, I had made a very important decision: If something was really wrong with
Chris and about to get worse, then despite my
parents' concern, I wasn't going to sit around and
do nothing. I had stopped a robbery, for heaven's
sake!

I vowed that, after school, I would catch the crosstown bus, I would walk into Appleton General Hospital,
and I would demand to see my brother. And when
they asked for identification, I would simply point to
the letters C.N. on my face mask and ask, "Whose
initials do you think these are?"

• • •

"They caught your bad guy!" Cecil grinned as I filed into class with him and JJ. He faked a drumroll, ending with a realistic-sounding cymbal crash—*"Bshhh!"*

"Now you can do interviews," JJ whispered loudly. "And you can tell the world about Captain Nobody and his sidekicks, and how we—"

"Please, JJ," I stopped her. "Please, don't."

The weary tone of my voice caused them to exchange a look.

"What's goin' on, man?" Cecil asked with friendly concern. But before I could answer, Mrs. Young called out, "Settle down! Settle down! We have some very special visitors this morning."

Everyone quickly took their seats, buzzing with curiosity.

"Our guests today are students at Fillmore High—isn't that exciting?" Mrs. Young announced, "Let's say hello to Fillmore's head cheerleader Colby Bryn and, from the Ferrets' championship football team, please welcome Darryl Peeps!"

In the final seconds of the Big Game, Darryl Peeps was the running back who had taken my brother's handoff and carried it halfway downfield before he got tackled. And Colby Bryn, dressed in her cheerleading outfit, looked even more awesome than she does at every football game.

"I'm going to let Colby and Darryl tell you why they're here," Mrs. Young said.

Colby tossed back her ponytail and began: "As many of you know, the Ferrets of Fillmore High School won the citywide football championship this past weekend. How cool is that?" She and Darryl pumped their fists and huffed, *"Whoo whoo whoo!"* A few of my classmates joined them.

Then she got serious. "But, as I'm sure you've probably heard, our quarterback Chris Newman got hurt in that game."

JJ and Cecil turned to see my reaction, but I stared straight ahead, chin up.

"Since Chris has been in the hospital," Darryl Peeps said, "everyone at Fillmore High School has been pulling for him, but we're also pretty bummed. And we know we're not the only ones who are feeling that way."

"No, we're not, Darryl," Colby continued, as if she was reading from a script they had both rehearsed. "We've been deeply touched by the support of people in our community, people like you and your families." She swept her arms open to include the whole class. "So the Spirit Squad came up with an idea that we thought would cheer everybody up during this difficult time. We decided to send our very own goodwill ambassador on tour."

"Please welcome our mascot . . ."—Darryl paused as he leaned out into the hallway and reentered with a large wire cage—". . . *Ferocious the Ferret!*"

I guess my classmates had never seen a ferret up

close before, because they all jumped up and oohed and aahed as they crowded around the cage on Mrs. Young's desk. I, however, stayed in my seat.

Chris has shown me Ferocious the Ferret before. He looks like a puzzled cat whose body has been stretched long and low to the ground. My brother once told me that even though ferrets are known for nipping hands and fingers, Ferocious had been trained to be pretty gentle. Before every football game, the cheerleading squad pulls Ferocious around the field perched on top of a wagon that everybody calls the Ferret Ferrari.

"We're called the Ferrets of Fillmore," Colby was explaining, "because ferrets are fighters. So to remind everybody of the fight that Chris Newman is putting up, we thought it would be a great idea to have Ferocious visit each classroom in Appleton Elementary School and spend a day with all you future Ferrets."

Mrs. Young gushed, "Isn't that exciting, everybody?"

"But that's not all!" Darryl boomed. "One of you is going to get an extra dose of Fillmore spirit, because one lucky student will get to take Ferocious home overnight!"

"Awesome!" a few kids exclaimed.

"And when that fortunate Ferret-in-training returns Ferocious tomorrow," Colby said, unrolling an official-looking scroll, "he—or she—will earn the title of 'Friend of Ferocious'!"

"Wow!" everyone sighed. Everyone, that is, except

Basher, who sniggered, "Who wants to be friends with a rat?" which of course made Evan McGee giggle.

Darryl held up a hand to signal for silence. "So now, the question is: Who will that special someone be?"

A forest of hands abruptly sprouted around Colby and Darryl. "Oooh! Me!" "No, me!" *"Pick me!"* kids chanted, getting louder and louder until suddenly a shrill whistle split the air.

Instantly, all noise stopped. Even Ferocious stood on his hind legs in his cage to see what kind of strange animal had made such a piercing sound.

Everyone turned to find Cecil with his fingers still in his mouth.

"Cecil!" Mrs. Young was irked. "Haven't we talked about that earsplitting talent of yours?"

"Sorry, but this is important," Cecil said. "I just don't think that there's any question about who that 'Friend of Ferocious' is supposed to be."

"Who?" asked a few dozen voices.

I cringed, because I knew what was coming next.

"It's gotta be Captain Nobody," Cecil said, pointing back to me, alone at my desk.

I saw a cloud of confusion pass over Colby's face, and I heard Darryl mutter, "Who's the kid in the costume?" Mrs. Young whispered to them, while my classmates nodded and exchanged shrugs. Suddenly Darryl exclaimed, "Are you serious?" and Colby added the inevitable "I didn't know Chris Newman had a younger brother."

• • •

Ferocious the Ferret turned out to be quite a distraction, because, throughout the day, my classmates were allowed to visit him in groups of three or four. Mrs. Young was constantly interrupting her lessons to remind kids to keep their fingers out of his cage and not to tease him, so we didn't get much class work done.

When the lunchtime bell rang, though, my classmates immediately forgot our furry visitor and rushed out, followed by Mrs. Young. I was left alone.

I wasn't hungry. Instead, I was worried. *How can I go to the hospital if I have to take Ferocious home for the night?*

I wandered over to Ferocious's cage, pulled up a chair and lowered my face to his level. "I bet you know my brother," I said. "Chris Newman? He's on the team."

Ferocious tilted his sleek little black-and-white head to one side and gazed into my eyes. Maybe he was just reacting to my mask, but for a second I thought that he might actually be hearing me. So I gulped, and because I couldn't think of anybody else I could say it to, I told Ferocious, "I want my brother back."

He made a chuckling sound, and then he went back to rolling around in his shredded newspaper. Right then, I felt totally lame for confiding my deepest wish to an animal. Even if he is a mascot.

By the end of the day, Cecil and JJ had figured out

that I wasn't exactly overjoyed about how they had volunteered me as a ferret babysitter, so they offered to keep me company on the way home.

"I thought I was doing you a favor," Cecil said as we left the school grounds.

I didn't answer. Ferocious's cage banged against my thigh with every step.

"Hey, think of it this way," he suggested. "Until your brother gets home, Ferocious can fill in for him. They're both Fillmore Ferrets, after all."

"So, what're you saying?" I snapped. "I don't get my brother back, but I get a fuzzy ferret instead?"

Cecil backed away. "Okay. Sorry I said anything."

"Look, I'm having a really bad week, okay?" I started to say. "So maybe you can understand why I'm not thrilled to be dragging Ferocious the Fillmore Ferret home . . ."

"Okay, Captain Nobody," Cecil tried to calm me.

"And I don't want to have to feed him dinner or clean up his poop . . ."

"Well, maybe one of us could take him," JJ suggested.

"Let me finish!" I snarled. "And I don't want to pretend like he's a replacement for my brother, because he's not."

"Of course he's not!" JJ agreed.

"My bad," Cecil shook his head. "How about I cut out my tongue?"

I knew he was trying to be funny, but I was in no

mood to laugh. Especially not when I looked up and saw Ricky Ratner and a half-dozen seventh-graders blocking our path.

Cecil and I froze. JJ reached into her shoulder bag and dug out the walkie-talkie.

"Should I call for help?" she whispered.

"Who you gonna call?" Cecil said out of the side of his mouth. "Captain Nobody's standing right here."

"Oh, right," she whimpered.

"I gave you an order!" Ricky Ratner barked as he and his posse approached. "You were supposed to tell your brother's classmates at Fillmore to stop hasslin' my cousin Reggie."

"Are they still doing stuff?" I asked.

"Don't act all innocent," Ricky scowled. "They're *torturing* him. People're callin' forty times a night and wakin' up the family. They order Chinese takeout and give Reggie's address. And last night, y'know what they did to the Charger?"

Everybody knows the Merrimac Charger. He's this huge bronze guy on horseback who towers over the front lawn of Merrimac High School.

"They painted 'Blame Reggie' all over it," Ricky yelled. "'*Blame Reggie!*' Your brother's friends did that!"

"But his *brother* didn't," Cecil shouted back, "cuz he's lying in a hospital!"

"Thanks to *your* cousin," JJ added.

"Nobody can prove that!" Ricky roared, bearing

down on me. "You show me *one* eyewitness who saw my cousin even come close to your . . . *yaaaaaaah!*"

Ricky recoiled at the sight of Ferocious, who—hearing all the noise—had suddenly reared up in his cage.

"What is *that*?" Ricky demanded. "Looks like a big, long rat."

His pals clustered around the cage as I pulled it to my chest.

"It's not a rat," JJ sniffed. "It's a ferret—a member of the weasel family."

"And this one's famous," Cecil boasted. "If you've ever been to a Fillmore football game—"

"I only cheer for cousin Reggie's school," Ricky snarled.

"Well, this one's name is Ferocious—"

I shot Cecil a warning look, but it was too late.

"'Ferocious'?" Ricky's eyebrows arched. "As in the Ferocious Ferrets of Fillmore?"

He waited for one of us to nod, but no one did.

"He's their mascot, right? Like the Charger of Merrimac?"

Cecil and I exchanged worried looks, and JJ tried to change the subject by exclaiming, "Ferocious is on a goodwill tour! I'm sure he'll be visiting the seventh grade any day now."

"Unless something unfortunate happens to him," Ricky taunted, looking around at his buddies. He gave a nod of his head, and suddenly everybody was trying to yank the cage out of my arms.

"Let go!" I yelled. "Stop it!"

JJ and Cecil tried to pull them off. "You don't want to mess with Captain Nobody," Cecil shouted, and JJ added, "This guy stopped a robbery yesterday! Don't you guys watch the news?"

But none of my attackers seemed impressed. They continued to scratch and claw at the cage, as poor Ferocious bounced back and forth from his water dish to his running wheel.

Suddenly, in the mad scramble, the cage door flew open and Ferocious shot up into the air. He landed on a patch of lawn, rolled over a few times and sat up, stunned by his newfound freedom.

Ferocious stared at us; we stared at him. And then, in a blink, Ferocious took off down the block like his tail was on fire.

Cecil, JJ and I screamed, "No, wait!" and raced after him. Behind us, Ricky and his buddies fell all over themselves with laughter.

As I ran, I dropped Ferocious's cage and threw off my backpack. JJ and Cecil tossed theirs aside, as well. We tore after my furry friend as he scampered across three front yards and then darted through a vegetable garden and under a thorny hedge. We tried to keep up, huffing and puffing and yelling, "Come back, Ferocious! Come back!"

We chased him down a dead-end street, where I thought we might have a chance of cornering him, but he ran down an embankment and through a wall of tall trees. We all tumbled down after him, and I fought my way through the trees to find myself at—*the highway!*

Ten feet in front of me, Ferocious had screeched to a halt on the shoulder of the road. I stopped, my pulse pounding. JJ and Cecil ran up alongside me, panting. We looked to each other in horrified silence as cars whizzed by, inches from Ferocious's twitching nose.

"Omigosh!" JJ gasped. "What're we gonna do?"

"Maybe we could lure him back this way," Cecil suggested in a low voice. "Does anybody have any raw meat?"

JJ and I looked at him, bewildered.

"Okay. Dumb question," he admitted. "But we shouldn't *all* go after him. That's only gonna freak him out."

"You know what this is, don't you?" JJ asked with great seriousness. "This is a job for Captain Nobody."

I almost gagged. "What?"

"She's right!" Cecil agreed. "After all, you're the one who got to take Ferocious home for the night."

"Only because you volunteered me!" I hissed.

"And look at him," JJ said. "It's like he's expecting you."

She was right. Sort of. Ferocious had been looking back at the three of us, but now he seemed to zero in on me. He tilted his head the way he had when I told him that I was Chris Newman's brother. In that moment, I felt very responsible for him.

Cecil clapped me on the back. "If anybody can do it, Captain Nobody can."

I took a deep breath. Locking eyes with Ferocious, I carefully inched my way across the narrow patch of gravel, fallen leaves and tree limbs that separated us. Ferocious watched me coming with a curious stare. *This just might work,* I thought as I drew near.

Just then, a passing motorist, who probably thought I was tiptoeing onto the asphalt, gave a warning toot on his horn.

I flinched, and Ferocious bolted. *Right out into traffic!*

Behind me, JJ and Cecil screamed. In front of me, four lanes of snorting cars seemed to chase Ferocious down the blacktop. My heart jumped to my throat, and I watched in horror as he dodged and bobbed, almost like my brother racing from the Merrimac football team on the night of the Big Game!

But unlike that night, I now had a chance to make a difference.

My inner other suddenly seemed to grab hold of the steering wheel in my brain. With my cape flying and my silver sneakers flashing, I dashed onto the blacktop. Frantically I waved my arms and screamed, "Stop! Stop!"

Traffic weaved around me, honking and screeching. Ferocious sped ahead until he reached the concrete barrier in the middle of the freeway, where he made a split-second hairpin turn, zipped between my legs and ran almost all the way back to where we began. I whirled and went after him.

Back and forth we sprinted as trucks and vans and cars whizzed dangerously close. *This is insane!* I thought as I ran for my life. *Is this what it's like for Chris in a football game?*

From the roadside, JJ was screaming, "Watch out! Watch out!!" while Cecil kept hooting, "Way to go, Captain Nobody!"

Once cars passed by me, they sped off down the highway. But as more drivers began to pump their brakes, the traffic coming at me and Ferocious began to slow down, and it backed up until, finally, all four lanes of traffic came to a stop. Ferocious and I had the freeway to ourselves.

He zigged and I zagged as the angry drivers leaned on their horns. The noise only made Ferocious more jumpy, and I kept tripping over myself as I darted back and forth, trying to catch up to him.

Just then a huge shadow passed over us.

Two massive wings suddenly blocked out the sun. At first I thought a humongous hawk had spotted Ferocious dashing around on the freeway and was swooping in to gobble him down for supper. But then I heard an engine sputtering.

I looked up and wilted in horror. A small airplane, coughing smoke from its engine, was headed straight for us, flying so low that its tires were practically rolling across the roofs of the stopped cars!

Without thinking, I dropped to the pavement and watched the belly of the plane as it passed overhead. I guess the angry drivers saw it, too, because their honking stopped. In the eerie quiet that followed, we could all hear the high-pitched squeal as the plane's tires hit the wide-open freeway up ahead. Its engine continued to belch black clouds of smoke as it taxied. Finally, way down the road, it came to a stop.

You could have heard a pin drop.

I looked behind me. Through their windshields, I saw the faces of all those drivers who, only moments before, had been cursing me and shaking their fists. Now they stared back with their mouths hanging open.

Then I looked down and saw the most amazing sight of all.

At my ankle sat Ferocious, also gazing in stunned fascination at the plane in the distance. I didn't hesitate. I reached down, scooped him up, and dashed for the roadside. As I blew by Cecil and JJ, I screamed, "I'll get you for this!"

18

IN WHICH
I LEARN AN
UNCOMFORTABLE TRUTH

We all wanted to stay and watch what happened next, but as a chorus of police sirens screamed closer and closer, Ferocious started scratching and nibbling at my hands. And once JJ reminded us how we'd thrown our backpacks and stuff all over the neighborhood, we reluctantly left.

First we ran back to find Ferocious's cage and put him in it. Then we all went back to my house, where we collapsed in the living room, still trembling from our terrifying adventure.

After a long, glassy-eyed silence, Cecil picked up the remote and turned on the TV, just as the five o'clock news was starting. Across the top of the screen, a red banner scrolled the words "Breaking News! Airplane Tragedy Averted!"

134

"What?" we all shouted in unison.

The newsman behind his desk was in the middle of announcing: ". . . and police are now saying that the freeway will be tied up for at least three more hours. For more on this amazing story, we take you to Mary Myron out on the Westside Highway. Mary?"

The picture switched to a shot of the newswoman— the same one who had reported from Sullivan's Jewelry Store the day before—standing in front of the plane that had almost lopped off my head. We all listened openmouthed as Mary Myron described the incident.

"A small passenger plane developed crippling engine trouble in the skies over Appleton this afternoon," she said. "As the pilot desperately searched for an unpopulated place to land, he spotted a stretch of freeway unexpectedly—some might even say, miraculously— cleared of cars."

"I couldn't believe my eyes!" the plane's pilot said, almost in tears. "It was like Moses parting the Red Sea, the way the lanes just opened up."

"We're famous! We're famous!" Cecil whooped.

"Cecil, please!" JJ shushed him. "I want to hear this."

"What—or who—brought traffic on the normally bustling Westside Highway to a standstill this afternoon?" Mary Myron continued. "Motorists who are bottled up in this massive traffic jam have some fascinating explanations."

"Some little bozo was out there, waving his arms and dancing around like he was trying to bring on the rain," said a red-faced bald man. "And you wouldn't believe the tribal costume he had on!"

I looked down at my rumpled clothes.

"He seemed to be chasing something," said a woman holding a baby on her shoulder, "but, from my car, I couldn't see what it was. I just assumed he was an escaped mental patient."

I winced.

"I don't care who that punk was or how many airplanes he saved," a tattooed truck driver was fuming, while behind him his rig sat immobilized in the tie-up. "If I get my hands on his neck, I'm gonna snap it."

I gulped.

The camera returned to Mary Myron. "Depending on who you speak to, the character who stopped traffic on the Westside Highway this afternoon is either a villain or a hero. Either way, the Appleton Police are *very* anxious to speak to him."

"That's *twice*!" JJ blurted. "Twice in two days you've been the lead story on the news."

"But you gotta get your picture on TV and in the papers, or else what's the use?" Cecil asked.

"He's right," JJ agreed. "Yesterday, the jewelry store cameras completely missed you, and today we left the scene too soon."

"Okay, here's what we've got to do." Cecil started to

pace around the living room. "We go back to the highway and introduce that TV lady to Captain Nobody. Then she'll interview you, and you'll talk about the Captain and his trusty sidekicks, and JJ and I will be standing by, so we can—"

"It's over," I said softly.

They both gasped. "What did you say?" asked JJ.

"You heard the TV. The police want me for questioning. People want to wring my neck, or they think I'm a mental patient. And maybe they're right." I tugged at my costume. "These clothes make me do crazy things."

"Not 'crazy'!" Cecil held up a finger of correction. *"Heroic."*

"Heroic, my foot," I scoffed. "I could've gotten shot yesterday . . ."

"But instead you stopped a robbery," JJ interjected.

". . . and today I missed getting run over about a hundred times."

"While you rescued people," Cecil said.

"And Ferocious," JJ added.

"My mom and dad are sick with worry, and what am I doing? Wearing a Halloween costume and pretending I can save the world, when I can't even . . ." I sighed. "I can't even save my own brother."

And, with that, I pulled off the mask, revealing my face for the first time that week.

"No, put it back on!" JJ wailed.

"You can't hang up your cape already!" Cecil cried.

"Sorry, guys." I shook my head sadly. "Captain Nobody is Captain no more."

• • •

After Cecil and JJ left, I looked at the clock and groaned. It was too late to catch the bus that would get me to Chris's hospital before visiting hours were over. Besides, I had a ferret to babysit. I trudged upstairs, feeling worse than I had all week.

In my bedroom, I took off the clothes I'd been wearing for the last four days. I studied the brightly colored garments in my hands and shook my head, bewildered that these few scraps of fabric had caused such bizarre behavior. Such insane daring! Such stupendous, amazing feelings of . . .

Stop!

It's over.

I balled up the clothes and stuffed them into a dresser drawer before I could be tempted to ever wear them again.

• • •

Around dinnertime, Dad called from the hospital.

"How's it going, Captain Nobody?" he asked.

"Actually, Dad," I said, "I think Captain Nobody's going back into a drawer."

"Oh," he answered. "If you say so." He sounded relieved, but we didn't talk about it anymore. Instead, he told me that he and Mom would be hanging out at the hospital, and could I make my own dinner?

"No prob," I assured him. This would have been the perfect time to ask him if what I'd read about Chris in the newspaper was true. But I was afraid to hear the answer to that question.

"And if I'm not home by the time you're in bed," Dad was wrapping up, "I'll catch you in the morning."

"Okay." I tried to sound cheerful. Before he could hang up, I blurted, "And Dad?"

"Yeah?" he answered.

"Tell Chris 'hi' for me."

Dad cleared his throat and snuffled before he said, "I'll do that, kiddo." And then he added a quiet "G'night, Newt."

I stood looking at the phone for a long time.

I wasn't hungry myself, but I fed Ferocious from a can of cat food that Darryl Peeps and Colby Bryn had given me. When he was done, I carried his cage upstairs and let him loose on the floor of my bedroom. He didn't show any interest in exploring, though. Instead, he jumped into my lap and shivered.

"I know," I murmured, stroking his long, slinky back. "That was pretty scary, huh?"

I could've sworn he nodded.

● ● ●

That night I dreamed I was back on the freeway, desperately dodging cars as I had done that afternoon, except that now every vehicle zooming toward me was painted either orange and green . . . or red and white.

Weird, I said to myself. *Those are Fillmore's and Merrimac's colors.* As soon as I made that realization, the cars' front hoods morphed into shiny plastic helmets, the cars' bodies became football players, and once again, my dream was a replay of the Big Tackle.

This time, though, everything was in slow motion. As Chris sailed into the end zone, behind him I could see all the players' faces through their face masks as they tumbled after him: Merrimac tacklers followed by Fillmore linemen, pulling each other down and slowly collapsing. And yet I could still see Chris's helmet, sticking out in front of the mountain of bodies that was piling on top of him.

Suddenly, soaring over the heap, here came . . . *Darryl Peeps?*

How'd he get downfield? Didn't he get tackled on the twenty-yard line? Apparently he had picked himself up and continued running, because here he was, flying up, up, up over the stack of bodies and then plunging down, down, down . . .

. . . until his helmet—*whomp!*—met my brother's.

"DARRYL PEEPS?" I shouted, and the next thing I knew, I was wide awake and breathing hard. From the floor next to my bed, Ferocious squeaked in his cage. I looked down to find him staring, as if demanding an explanation for my outburst.

"It wasn't Reggie Ratner," I whispered. "I remember now. I saw it happen. Darryl Peeps put Chris in a coma!"

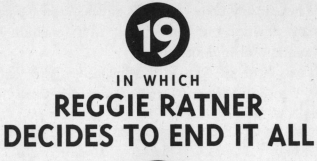

IN WHICH
REGGIE RATNER
DECIDES TO END IT ALL

For the rest of the night I tossed and turned, and when I finally stumbled down to breakfast in my blue jeans and a short-sleeved shirt, I found Mom puttering around the kitchen. She looked like she hadn't slept well either.

"G'mornin', sunshine," she said hoarsely. Just then, the toaster popped up two pieces of bread, and Mom flinched.

"Now, who put those in there?" she wondered.

"It wasn't me," I mumbled. I kissed her on the cheek and set the ferret cage on the butcher block.

"My stars!" Mom exclaimed, peering in. "Is that Ferocious?"

"Sure is."

"Did you two have a sleepover?"

"It's a long story," I groaned. "But he's going back today."

She looked me up and down.

"It's good to see your face again." She smiled.

When she turned away to butter her toast, I took a deep breath and said gently, "I read what that doctor thinks. About Chris having six days before we'd have to worry."

Mom stopped buttering and slowly set down her knife.

"And today's the sixth day?"

She nodded.

"Are you worried?"

Mom squeezed her lips like she was wrestling with the words in her mouth, and then she said, "We're . . . hopeful."

For a long moment it was so quiet I could hear the ticking of the kitchen clock. Then I surprised us both by announcing:

"I'm coming to see him after school."

• • •

When I ran up to my bedroom to grab my backpack, I caught sight of myself in the mirror. I had forgotten how small and skinny I look in everyday clothes. I know I vowed never to wear that costume again, but even so, I opened my dresser drawer and ran my hand over Captain Nobody's clothes. Just touching them made me feel less upset about Chris. More powerful somehow.

And that's why I stuffed them into my backpack before I dashed out of the house.

In the school yard, a bunch of kids crowded around to peer through the bars of the ferret cage. Basher poked at Ferocious with a twig.

"Hey, c'mon, Basher," I said, "don't hurt him."

Basher sneered, "And who's gonna stop me?"

It was a valid question. Without the security of the Captain Nobody mask, I suddenly felt very vulnerable. I didn't have to answer, though, because JJ and Cecil joined me at that moment, and Basher scoffed and wandered back into the school yard crowd.

Cecil frowned as he regarded my street clothes.

"What?" I asked.

"I'm not gonna lie," he shrugged. "I miss Captain Nobody."

I looked to JJ. "Do you?"

She crinkled her nose. "When I was five, y'know? I woke up one morning and announced that my name was now Princess Zarzuela and that, because I was of royal birth, I would never brush my hair again, and I would only eat white foods. For one whole week, I ate rice and milk and bread with the crusts cut off, and my hair got so wiry and tangled that I started to pick up radio signals. The morning after that happened, I announced that I was JJ again. So . . . you don't have to explain to me."

I nodded, grateful for the support.

"You know what?" Cecil asked, looking between me and JJ. "You guys are two cups of crazy."

• • •

I thought that my new appearance—or rather, my *old* appearance—might trigger more comments from my classmates, but they didn't seem to notice one way or the other. They just ignored me the way they always had. Even after I returned the ferret cage to Mrs. Young and she presented me with a scroll naming me a "Friend of Ferocious," they were unimpressed.

"Well, whoop-de-doo," Basher teased as I passed him on my way back to my desk.

"I want Ferocious next," a voice called out, and that was the cue for everyone to wag their hands and chime in: "No! It's my turn!" "I want him!" "Me me me me me!"

I returned to my desk and looked up to find Ferocious still watching me through his bars. *You're just going to leave me?* he seemed to be saying. *After all we've been through?*

He had a point. In the single day I'd had custody of him, we had faced death together, and I had told him my two biggest secrets—how badly I missed Chris, and how Darryl Peeps was the one who had hit my brother. Those were secrets I hadn't even shared with JJ and Cecil. And they were supposed to be my friends.

Geez. At this moment, my best friend is a ferret. And although I was surrounded by a room full of people, I'd never felt so alone.

• • •

On the way to lunch, I passed Principal Toomey, who was deep in conversation with Mr. Brockman, our guidance counselor.

"Hey, Mr. Toomey, Mr. Brockman," I waved.

They nodded quickly and continued walking. "And what's that student's name?" I heard Mr. Toomey grumble as they passed.

"Beats me," Mr. Brockman replied.

Right about then the sirens began. A single wail started in the distance, but it was quickly joined by many more. The racket grew deafening as police cars and ambulances and fire trucks zoomed past our school and howled down Broad Street.

JJ and Cecil rushed past in a tidal wave of students racing out to watch the emergency vehicles go by.

"What's happening?" I shouted.

"Probably something awful," Cecil said excitedly.

I spotted a lot of teachers hurrying into the faculty lounge, so I peered in the doorway and found them all crowded around the TV. Mrs. Marcus, the school nurse, exclaimed, "Oh, will you look at that poor, tortured boy!" just as, from the television, I heard, "The victim is identified as Reggie Ratner."

Reggie Ratner? I thought. *A victim? Of what?*

I climbed on a chair at the back of the lounge to get a look at the TV over the teachers' heads.

"I'm standing at the base of the Appleton water tower, the tallest structure in town," the reporter Mary Myron was explaining as, all around her, emergency vehicles screeched up, sirens wailing and lights flashing. "Sometime early this morning, Merrimac High School senior and celebrated football player Reggie Ratner climbed onto the roof of this tower in what authorities fear is a suicide attempt."

I practically toppled off the chair. *Suicide? Why would Reggie want to do that?*

"Why, you might ask," Mary Myron continued, as if she'd heard the voice in my head. "Why would this young man want to harm himself? This question is on the minds of the many people gathering here right now."

A camera shot showed a single figure sitting, sad and alone, way up on the conical roof of the tower.

"From our conversations with Reggie's parents, classmates and teachers," Mary Myron said, "we've learned this much: For the last week, Reggie Ratner has grown increasingly depressed as students and fans of Fillmore High School have repeatedly harassed him and his family."

That's what this is about? I wondered. *Kids dumped garbage on his lawn, so he's going to kill himself?*

"Apparently, those Fillmore students accuse Reggie,

a successful defensive end, of delivering the critical blow that knocked popular Fillmore football star Chris Newman unconscious at last Friday night's championship game."

He didn't! I wanted to shout. *It was Darryl Peeps!*

I jumped down from the chair and stumbled out into the hallway. My legs were shaky. This was terrible! Somebody had to tell Reggie that it wasn't his fault. But who could do that?

After all, I was the only person who knew the truth.

20

IN WHICH

I CLIMB UP TO THE SKY

As I wandered down the empty hall, my mind was churning. Who could I tell about Darryl Peeps? It would have to be somebody who could get Reggie Ratner's attention, somebody with enough authority to convince him to give up his dangerous plan and to come down off his tower.

I thought about Dad; he's good at getting people to listen. But he and Mom were pretty tied up at the moment.

How about Chris's teammates? Weren't they the ones who had been torturing Reggie all week? Maybe, I thought, I could race over to Fillmore High School, burst into the football players' classrooms and tell them exactly what I had remembered about the Big

Tackle. Then they would rush to the water tower and shout apologies up to Reggie, wouldn't they?

But what if they didn't believe me?

Or what if they accused me of betraying my brother by blaming Darryl and siding with Reggie?

Or what if all of that took too much time?

Who else? Mr. Toomey?

No.

Mrs. Young?

No.

Somebody else. *Anybody else!!*

Then it hit me: There was nobody else. Because nobody else had seen what I had seen, and nobody else was Chris Newman's younger brother, and nobody else could deliver the news that might make Reggie Ratner reconsider his jump.

• • •

After I'd breathlessly told Cecil and JJ what I had to do, Cecil screwed up his face. "Okay, once you get to the water tower," he wondered, "how're you going to talk to Reggie?"

I had no answer.

"I bet somebody'll have a bullhorn," JJ suggested.

"That's it!" I said. "I'll use a bullhorn!"

"So you're gonna walk up to a policeman," Cecil said, "and say, 'Hey, officer, let me use your bullhorn, because I want to tell Reggie Ratner about a dream I had'?"

"Oooh, yeah," I winced. "That probably won't work."

"How's this?" Cecil proposed. "I got a cousin in the Navy who showed me how they flash light signals from ship to ship with mirrors. It is so awesome."

"Do you know the code?" JJ asked him.

"Well. No."

"And, even if *you* did, what are the chances that Reggie would know the code?" she continued.

"Okay, okay, you made your point!" He clapped me on the shoulder. "Seems to me the only way you're going to get Reggie Ratner's attention is to sit down and talk to him, man to man."

"How?" I exploded. "He's on the roof of the tallest building in town!"

"Which means," JJ reasoned, "that there must be a ladder that goes all the way to the top." She noticed my shudder. "Oh, I forgot. You're scared of heights."

"Petrified."

"It's no big deal," JJ assured me. "I'm afraid of spiders."

"Me?" Cecil scrunched up his shoulders in fear. "Plastic garbage bags."

"Garbage bags?" JJ looked surprised. "Why?"

"They're . . . *slimy*," Cecil winced.

"Is that why you sent me into the Dumpster to get your drum?" I asked.

Cecil shrugged. "Guilty as charged." He snapped his fingers. "Hey, wait a sec! You had no problem climbing up on that garbage pile. And that was pretty high."

"Yeah, but that wasn't me," I moaned. "That was . . . well, you know . . ." My voice trailed off.

"Yeah," said Cecil slyly. "We sure *do* know who that was."

"And we all know what he's capable of," JJ added, stressing every word.

They folded their arms and waited.

"No," I shook my head. "Uh-uh. No way."

But they kept staring until I had to accept that they were right. And when I did, my stomach flipped like a pancake.

● ● ●

In the boys' bathroom, I pulled the Captain Nobody costume from my backpack. A thrill ran up my spine as I slipped it on, tied up the silver sneakers and tugged the mask down over my nose. It felt like being reunited with a long-lost friend.

"Oh, yeah," I exhaled.

I tiptoed down a back stairway and exited into the faculty parking lot, where JJ and Cecil had pulled up on their bikes. When they saw me, their mouths flew open.

"Shhhh!" I warned, holding a finger to my lips.

"He's back!" Cecil whispered excitedly.

"You're gonna get in trouble for cutting," I reminded them. "You're sure you want to do this?"

"Are you kidding?" JJ gasped. "This is what side-kicks do!"

I climbed onto Cecil's crossbar and we all sped off, using the police helicopter in the distance as a guide for our journey across town. Once we got close to the Appleton water tower, we drove around the mob of people and all the emergency vehicles and news vans gathering in front.

Since the wobbly old tower had been condemned about five years ago, a wire fence had been erected around the entire block, and weeds and vines had grown up so high on all sides that you could lose a basketball team in there. Over time, trespassers had cut a few patches of fence here and there and peeled them open, so once we got to the back of the tower and dropped the bikes behind some bushes, we found a flap that we could all squeeze through. Inside the fence, we squatted in the weeds and surveyed the situation.

Cecil nudged us and indicated the ladder that ran up a leg of the water tower to the roof. The rusting brackets that held the ladder onto the rickety tower were pulling away. Discolored screws stuck out of the rotting wood, and, in a few places, the rungs of the ladder were snapped in two. Even worse, the first solid rung was about six feet off the ground.

"I can't reach the first rung!" I whispered frantically.

"I'll give you a boost," JJ offered. "I'm the tallest."

"But what about the rungs above it?" I pointed out. "They look about as sturdy as celery."

"Then it's a good thing you don't weigh anything," Cecil said.

"Let's not stand around yakking," JJ hissed. "We've got company."

She jerked her head toward a policeman who was wrapping the fence with yellow plastic tape that said POLICE LINE—DO NOT CROSS. In about ten seconds he would get close enough to see us through the weeds.

"Get ready to rock and roll, Captain," Cecil whispered. He grabbed two sticks from the ground and skittered back through the fence, where he stood up and let loose a drum riff along the chain link, finishing with a vocal cymbal crash. "*Ksssh!*"

The startled cop looked up. "Hey!" he yelled. "What're you doing?"

"Me? I'm a parade!" Cecil crowed, just before he sprinted off.

The cop blinked in confusion—"Huh?"—before he dashed after Cecil, shouting, "Come back here!" and trailing a long plastic ribbon behind himself.

"Let's go!" JJ grabbed my hand and pulled me toward the foot of the ladder. She folded her fingers into a stirrup and held them down for me to put my foot into.

"Remind me," I pleaded with a dry throat, "why am I doing this?"

"Because there's a human life at stake," she explained calmly, "and that makes this a job for Captain Nobody."

I gulped. Holding on to JJ's shoulders, I stepped into her hands, and she boosted me up to the lowest unbroken rung. She pushed from below as I pulled myself up. I reached for the next rung. And the next. And the next.

As I feared, a few of the rotting rungs were broken, and even the unbroken ones creaked when I grabbed them. Nevertheless, they held my weight as I climbed up. Luckily, from behind my mask all I could see was the ladder. I couldn't see the sky soaring above. Or the earth dropping away below.

The sounds from the ground—the sirens and horns and shouts from the crowd—gradually faded and were replaced with the drone of the helicopter circling the tower. Just before I reached the edge of the roof, it swooped past, and a wallop of wind slammed me against the ladder. I wrapped my arms around the uprights and held on tight until the hurricane had passed.

Unfortunately, when I hugged the ladder, my mask hooked on a jutting nail. So when I reached up to hoist myself onto the roof, I felt a tug, and my mask was ripped from my face.

"Oh, *no!*" I cried, turning my head to watch the fabric flutter down . . .

. . . down . . .

. . . down.

I shouldn't have done that. Because way down below the still-falling mask I could see JJ. Who looked about as big as the period at the end of this sentence.

I gagged and gripped the ladder. Not only was I about a bazillion miles above earth, but, without my mask, I wasn't Captain Nobody anymore! What was *Newt Newman* going to do now?

I considered a retreat, a slow descent down the rotting ladder. My teeth chattered in fear at the thought.

I considered not moving. The police would eventually see my predicament—wouldn't they?—and send a helicopter, throw me a rope and lower me to safety.

But then I considered Reggie Ratner, all alone and desperate. So I pulled myself over the edge of the roof and lay there, panting.

After the first wave of cold, white terror passed through my body, I carefully raised my head and looked around. Below me, Appleton stretched out in every direction. The trees and buildings and streets looked like they belonged in the candy village that goes on exhibit every Christmas at the Three Rivers Mall.

Wow, I thought, *this is kind of awesome,* but in the next second I remembered where I was. I shuddered and dug my fingernails into the shingles.

The water tower's circular roof was shaped like a stubby, upside-down ice-cream cone, so that, from the edges, it rose to a point where an old weather vane still creaked in the wind.

I had just pulled myself to my knees when the police helicopter swooped in for a closer look and its downdraft flattened me against the shingles.

How am I supposed to move now? I shrieked inside my skull.

And then I remembered Sticky Ricky.

Sticky Ricky was a crimefighter I once created whose body was covered with hundreds of tiny suction cups that enabled him to slither up steel walls and towers of glass.

"I can slither," I said aloud.

Fighting the wind from the helicopter, I very slowly inched up the rooftop on my belly until I saw Reggie Ratner on the opposite edge. I'd never seen Reggie out of his football uniform, but there was no mistaking the guy. His neck and arms were as thick as Chris had always joked about. He was sitting with one knee pulled up to his chest and the hood of a sweatshirt flipped over his head as he watched the crowd on the ground below.

The helicopter veered away, but even though I was no longer pinned down, I stayed on my stomach, wiggling down the slope of the roof until I was just behind Reggie. I guess I should have coughed or something to warn him that I was there, because when I gently called, "Reggie?" he shrieked, "Nyahhh!" and practically tumbled off the roof. He twisted around and glared at me.

"Hi," I said and gave a little wave.

"What d'you think you're . . . ?" he sputtered. "How did you even . . . *Who are you?*"

"I'm Newt Newman?" I said. "Chris Newman's younger brother?"

"You're joking!" Reggie snorted. "I didn't even know Chris *had* a younger brother."

"That's okay," I sighed. "Nobody does."

"Hmm. Weird," Reggie said. "How is Chris?"

"He's still . . . out."

"Man," Reggie shook his head sadly, "that sucks."

And y'know what? In that moment, I liked him. Because of his long rivalry with Chris, I guess I had always imagined that Reggie Ratner was some knuckle-dragging, heartless jerk. Instead, he seemed sincerely bummed out about my brother.

"But what're you doing here?" he asked. "And what're you wearing?"

"Can we talk about the clothes later?" I said, edging a little closer. "Right now, I . . . I have to talk to you about something important."

"Are you nuts?" Reggie cried. "What could be so important that you'd—"

"I know you didn't knock out my brother!"

Reggie stared at me.

"I was there, outside the end zone fence," I explained. "I saw everything. Chris was hit by Darryl Peeps's helmet. You weren't anywhere close."

"Thank you!" Reggie shouted. "That's what I've been trying to tell people all week! Especially your

brother's teammates. But they came after me anyway."
He looked away and sighed. "It's been bad."

"I know," I said. "I go to the same school as your
cousin Ricky . . ."

"Oh, yeah?" Reggie brightened. "You're friends with
Ricky?"

"We've, uh . . . met," I said. "He told me what
you've been going through, and I'm really sorry about
all that."

Reggie squinted in confusion. "Wait . . . You climbed
up here to apologize?"

"Not exactly," I said, trying to choose my words
carefully. "I came because I'm the only person who
knows the truth, so I'm the only person who can
change your mind."

"Change my mind? About what?"

It was right then that I noticed something weird.
Sticking out of the pockets of Reggie's hoodie were a
couple of cans of spray paint with orange and green
caps. Orange and green? Merrimac's school colors?

I blurted, "You're not up here to jump, are you?"

Reggie blinked. "What?"

"You came up to spray 'Go Merrimac!' or something
like that on the water tank, didn't you?"

"Why else would I be here?"

"People on the ground are saying that you got so
depressed from being hassled all week that you climbed
up here to . . ." I joined my hands and made a diving
motion. "And I thought I could talk you out of it."

"They think I'm up here to kill myself?"

I nodded.

"Oh, please!" Reggie scoffed.

Suddenly a voice crackled through a bullhorn way down below us.

"REGGIE RATNER? THIS IS SERGEANT SCHMALZ OF THE APPLETON POLICE DEPARTMENT. LISTEN, SON, WE KNOW YOU'VE BEEN THROUGH A LOT LATELY, BUT I WOULD JUST ASK YOU TO REMEMBER THAT YOU'RE YOUNG, AND YOU'VE GOT YOUR WHOLE LIFE AHEAD OF YOU."

Reggie whirled toward me, his eyes bugging. "They think I'm up here to kill myself!"

"In a nutshell."

"Oh, no! What a mess!" He ran his fingers through his hair. "What a big, stinking pile of mess." He looked me in the face. "Newton? Can I tell you what really happened?"

I nodded.

"Ever since the Big Game," he began, "people have been coming down on me from all sides. All those jerks from Fillmore. People on the street. Even my classmates! The world hates me, my reputation is shot, my stomach's in knots 24/7. So finally I made a decision. I had to do something I'd be remembered for besides knocking out Chris Newman . . . *which I didn't even do!*"

"I know, I know."

"So, I got up here early this morning, with my paint

and my rope." He held up a coil of rope I hadn't seen before. "And I was all set to lower myself over the edge, and then *this* happened!" He pulled back a corner of his jacket to reveal that his left foot was stuck through a hole in the shingles.

"Wow," I said, studying the opening. "You stomped a hole in the roof."

"I was just walking," he insisted, "but this roof . . . this whole tower . . . it's rotted clear through. I wish somebody had told me."

"Maybe that's why it's condemned?" I suggested.

"Maybe," he shrugged. "It probably doesn't help that I weigh two-eighty. Plus I had seven bagels for breakfast."

I wriggled closer and peered through the hole his foot had made.

"Looks like your shoe's stuck between two beams."

"It's more than stuck . . . it's, like, wedged," he sighed. "And when I brace myself and try pulling it out, I only end up breaking off more of these shingles. When the cops first came, I thought they'd send a guy up. Or maybe the fire department would raise a ladder. But, nah, they know this place is falling apart. I mean, who's gonna be stupid enough to climb up here?"

I almost raised my hand, but that's when Sergeant Schmalz belched through his bullhorn, "IT'S NOT WORTH IT, SON!" and we both flinched.

"I CAN ASSURE YOU THAT THE CITIZENS OF AP-

PLETON ARE WILLING TO FORGIVE WHAT YOU DID TO CHRIS NEWMAN . . ." But then his voice was drowned out by a horrendous roar as the police helicopter was now joined by three more choppers from local TV stations. They crisscrossed the sky, making my cape flap wildly around my head.

Reggie shouted above the roar, "Can you help me?"

"I-I don't see how I could," I stuttered.

"But you're my only hope!" he pleaded.

I thought long and hard before I said, "I maybe have one idea."

"What? What? I'll try anything!"

"Untie your shoe and pull your foot out of it."

"Don't you think I tried that already?" Reggie hollered. "Yeesh!"

I squinted into the hole. "But your shoe is still tied."

"Well, that's only because I . . . I triple-knotted the shoelace," he stammered, embarrassed. "And with these fingers"—he held up hands the size of skillets—"I can't untie it."

"It also doesn't help that you bite your nails," I pointed out.

"You sound like my mother," he scowled.

"Let me see what I can do."

I edged closer and reached through the hole in the roof. At first, my fingernails chipped on the tightly knotted cord. After just a few minutes, my fingertips were rubbed raw and my hands started shaking from exhaustion. But little by little the loops started to loosen.

"I made it too tight, didn't I?" Reggie wailed in despair.

"Yeah, you did," I said, still facedown. "But try pulling your foot out now."

"Are you serious?" Reggie asked, startled.

"Pull!" I yelled.

With a single grunt, Reggie slid his foot from the shoe, which tumbled down into the blackness of the empty water tank we were sitting over.

"You did it!" Reggie yelled, wiggling his toes and rubbing his foot. "You're a genius." He started to stand.

"Don't move!" I ordered.

"I wanna get outta here."

"If you walk back across the roof, you could make more holes, and the roof could cave in. Then we'd both end up where your shoe is right now."

He sat back down, fuming. "So, okay, how do you suggest I get from here to the ladder?"

"You need to crawl."

"Crawl?" Reggie exploded. "That's really why you're here, isn't it? I haven't been humiliated enough, and now you won't be happy until you see me—"

"Reggie!" I shouted. "You have to lie on your belly and . . . slither. Like Sticky Ricky."

"Who's Sticky Ricky?"

"Just do it!" I barked.

"All right, all right," Reggie grumbled. "I'll slither."

He followed my example and lay facedown. Like soldiers squirming under barbed wire, we wriggled across the roof to the ladder without punching a single hole.

The news helicopters seemed to get very excited by our journey. They droned closer, like humongous, curious bumblebees. Through their Plexiglas bubbles, I could see reporters following all of our moves with video cameras. *We're on TV,* I thought. *We're being seen all over Appleton.*

Once I got into position at the top of the ladder, I yelled above the copter noise, "Reggie? You wait here."

He grabbed my arm. "You're not going to leave me, are you?"

I leaned close to his ear. "I don't think this ladder can take our combined weight," I tried to explain calmly. "So you have to hold off till I'm at the bottom before you start down. Can you do that?"

He gulped and nodded nervously.

"And the middle of the rung is the weakest part," I said, "so be sure to step on the far edges. Okay?"

"Yeah, yeah, yeah," he jabbered, anxious for me to get going so that he could follow.

I swung a leg over the roof's edge and found the first step. With great care, I set my feet and eased my weight onto each descending rung. I found that it helped to count, *"One, one-thousand, two, one-thousand, three, one-thousand"* between each move.

I've got rhythm! I smiled. *Cecil would be so proud of me.*

When I got to "nine, one-thousand," though, I stopped counting. A tremor in the ladder grew to a shudder, and the rusty braces screwed to the water tower's supports began to groan. *What's happening?*

I looked up quickly and was met with the sight of Reggie Ratner's butt as he swung himself off the roof and began his descent.

"No, Reggie!" I screamed. I'm sure he was freaking out all alone up there, but what part of "Wait!" hadn't he understood?

To make matters worse, one of Reggie's feet snapped a rung, sending pieces of wood tumbling around me. I winced and tried to dodge the debris, but my gyrations only added to the herky-jerky motion of the ladder. To steady myself, I put both feet onto the same rung, which immediately shattered, leaving me dangling in space!

Frantically, I bicycled my legs, trying to find a surface, any surface. And I might have been able to regain my balance if it weren't for that last, unexpected chunk of Reggie's rung that bonked me in the middle of the forehead. I was so startled that my hands popped open.

"Huh?" I grunted.

And I fell.

• • •

It's amazing how fast a brain can operate in times of intense stress. Like I told you, I've been falling for what seems like hours—well, certainly enough time to bring you up to speed on my story—and I still haven't hit the ground.

Isn't this where you came in?

21

IN WHICH
I FINISH FALLING

Like the folding of a pirate's spyglass, time collapsed in on me, and I was suddenly dropping so fast that I left the scream I was screaming somewhere far above my body. I was pure motion, tumbling, tumbling, eyes wide open in terror as everything rushed together.

There's the sky!

Then the ground!

Sky!

Ground!

Skygroundskygroundskygroundsky . . .

A blue pillow rushed up to greet me and—

WHOOMPH!

I was swallowed by a massive, inflated rubber mattress.

I was on the ground, and I was alive!

"Yahoo!" I was about to holler, except that the word caught in my throat when I looked up to find that Reggie Ratner—two hundred and eighty pounds of muscle and seven bagels, too—was plunging down on top of me!

In a blink, he blotted out the sun. In the next tick-tock, he landed on me, driving me into the blue mattress with a powerful *WHUMP!*

All the breath—*OOF!*—was pushed from my body.

A lightning bolt of red-hot pain—*ZING!*—ripped up my right leg.

And, just as the darkness behind my eyelids erupted with about a thousand shooting stars, I passed out.

22

IN WHICH
I FINALLY GET TO THE HOSPITAL

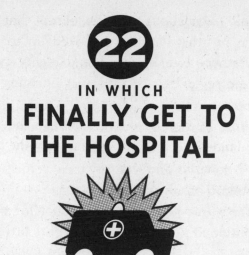

I opened one eye. The fluorescent lights on the ceiling were blindingly bright. My right leg and chest were throbbing with pain. I squeezed a fist and found that someone's hand was holding mine.

"Newt?" It was my mom's voice. She was standing over me, stroking my head and calling over her shoulder. "Honey, he's awake!"

Dad joined her and laid a hand on my chest. Their faces were twisted with concern. "I'm fine," I tried to assure them, but my voice cracked with the effort. "No, really," I tried again.

They both laughed a little. "Is Reggie okay?" I croaked.

"Not a scratch," Dad said. "You broke his fall."

"And he broke your ankle and two ribs," Mom added.

"Oh." So *that's* where the pain was coming from. "Where am I now?"

"In a recovery room," Mom said, indicating a white curtain that bordered my bed. "The doctors taped your ribs and put a cast on your foot. See?"

I looked down to find that my toes were sticking out of a mountain of white plaster.

"And the nurse just gave you a shot for the pain," Mom continued, "so you might feel a little drowsy, but—"

"Wait a minute!" I cried out. *"I'm at the hospital?"* I tried to rise up on one elbow, but a huge jolt of pain smacked me back onto the mattress.

"Try to lie still, sweetie," Mom cautioned.

"But if I'm at the hospital, can I visit Chris?" I asked excitedly.

"You boys are going to be sharing a room," Dad said.

"Really?"

"At this point, the doctors say it's okay," Mom said.

My heart started double-thumping. After a whole week, I'd finally get to see my—

Hold on.

What was *that*?

Behind my parents' heads, in a corner of the room, a television hung suspended from the ceiling. Although

I was groggy, I could swear that on the screen I was seeing . . .

"Cecil?" I squinted. "Is that Cecil on TV?"

"Oh, yeah," Dad laughed, turning to look. "He and JJ are doing interviews on every channel in town."

"What for?"

"Somebody has to explain how Captain Nobody got mixed up in the most daring rescue in Appleton history!" Mom declared proudly.

"Huh?"

"We'd better start at the beginning," Dad said.

"Apparently," Mom began, "only one TV station was covering the Reggie Ratner story at first."

"But when you climbed onto the roof," Dad said, "the media went wild! Every station in the county sent news crews and helicopters . . ."

"Oh, I saw the helicopters," I groaned.

". . . and they all interrupted their regular programming to switch over to the water tower. And suddenly, there you were, on the TV in Chris's hospital room. Your mother and I couldn't believe our eyes!"

"Can you imagine how scared I was?" Mom asked.

"I have a pretty good idea," I muttered.

"And while you were up there," Dad continued, "lots more people rushed to the tower. Hundreds!"

"By the time we jumped in the car and tried to drive over," Mom explained, "we couldn't get within a half mile of the place. The streets were gridlocked, so we pulled over and tried to go the rest of the way on foot.

But just as we got close to the tower . . ."—her voice faltered—". . . just as we arrived . . ."

Dad put an arm around her shoulder.

"We got there in time to see you fall," he explained.

Mom raised a trembling hand to wipe her eyes.

"I'm sorry," I said.

"Don't be silly!" Dad laughed. "You're okay, and that's all that matters."

"Fortunately, I was able to join you in the ambulance," Mom said, "and your father drove the car."

"And by the time I got back here," Dad said, "you were all over the news."

"Really?"

"Really! You in your Captain Nobody suit . . . that's all anybody is talking about."

"Remember that nice Mr. Clay, the locksmith I always used?" Mom asked. "Well, he phoned a radio program and said that he recognized your costume. He remembered your name was Captain Nobody and that you had helped him find his house when he recently got lost. Is this true?"

I shrugged. "He just ran out of his medicine."

"Next thing you know," Dad said, "that lovely Irish couple Mr. and Mrs. Sullivan called a TV crew to their jewelry store because *they* had been watching the news and wanted to tell the world how Captain Nobody had prevented a robbery at their shop." He smacked his forehead. "You stopped a robbery and you never said a word about it?"

Before I could explain, Mom jumped in. "Did you know the thief had a gun?" she gasped. "You could have been hurt!"

"It was right about then," Dad went on, "when all the reporters started wondering, 'Who is this mysterious Captain Nobody?'"

"And that's the first time we saw JJ and Cecil on the air," giggled Mom. "They were so funny! Cecil grabbed the poor reporter's microphone to explain that Captain Nobody was actually Chris Newman's younger brother . . ."

". . . and the reporter had the gall to say, 'I didn't know Chris Newman had a younger brother!'" Dad fumed. "Do you believe that?"

Then Mom blew up. "And what were you doing on the freeway yesterday?"

"Why?" I tried to sound innocent. "What are they saying?"

"Dozens of people are now telling the police how they saw Captain Nobody stop traffic on the Westside Highway!" Mom wailed. "What have I told you about playing in the street?"

"And that plane that made an emergency landing?" Dad exclaimed. "They're saying you saved lives!"

"I-I was just trying to save Ferocious," I stammered.

"Ferocious? The ferret?" Dad asked. "What were you doing with—"

"They had a sleepover," Mom interrupted, patting his arm.

"Oh. Well, you've had one heck of a week, Newt. Why haven't you said anything?"

"You guys were kind of . . . busy," I said meekly.

Outside my curtain voices suddenly started shouting:

"Yo, Reggie! How 'bout a photo?"

"Reggie, what did you think about as you faced death?"

"Hey, Reggie! You gonna visit Chris Newman while you're here?"

We all looked up to find Reggie Ratner standing at the foot of my bed. Through the open curtain behind him, I could see a crush of reporters clustered outside the sliding glass doors of the recovery room, all wagging microphones and pointing cameras in Reggie's direction. They were held back by a line of security guards who had locked arms.

"Hey," he mumbled, and closed the curtain behind himself.

"Hey, Reggie," I waved weakly. "Did you meet my parents?"

He raised a hand in greeting, and they nodded curtly. I figured that maybe they were still sore about Reggie's role in the Big Tackle.

"Oh, just so you know," I said, "Reggie didn't knock out Chris."

Dad's eyes flew open. "Excuse me?"

"I was there. I saw it. It was Darryl Peeps."

"Darryl Peeps?" Dad sounded confused.

"I swear. It just took me a while to remember. So don't blame Reggie for what happened to Chris, okay?"

"Even so," Mom said sourly, "he *did* land on you."

"Well, yeah," I admitted, "there's that."

"Could I, uh, talk to you?" Reggie asked me.

"We'll get some coffee," Mom said. As she and Dad passed Reggie, I heard Dad whisper, "You might want to start with 'I'm sorry.'"

When they exited the recovery room, the glass doors slid open again and the questions and shouts from the reporters built to a frenzy. But once the doors closed, the uproar subsided.

Reggie moved up to the head of my bed.

"How you doin'?" he said.

"I don't really know," I shrugged. "They gave me a pain shot."

"Oh." He looked to the ceiling for a moment, before drawing a deep breath. "Okay, here's the deal: I'm sorry. Seriously. I never meant for anybody else to get involved, y'know? But I totally appreciate how you helped me out. So, thanks. Okay?"

I shrugged. "I just untied your shoe."

"Yeah, about two hundred feet in the air." He leaned close and whispered, "One more thing: You won't tell anybody about the spray paint, right?"

"Huh?"

"I mean, all this fuss? All because of a senior prank?" he scoffed. "It'd make me look like such a loser."

"So you'd rather let everybody assume you were up there to jump?"

"To *think*," he corrected me. "I'm telling people I went up there cuz I needed to *think*. Since I've been, y'know . . . *upset*."

"Oh, right," I said slowly. "You've been upset."

He held up a fist for me to punch as a show of agreement. "Our secret?"

I studied his face, so massive and muscled. And so afraid. *I guess I'm not the only one who gets scared,* I thought.

I raised my arm, bristling with tubes and needles, made a fist, and bopped his. "Our secret."

Reggie sighed with gratitude.

• • •

By the time my plaster cast was dry, the mob of gawkers and reporters had grown to the size of a small suburb. As the nurses wheeled me out of the emergency room, they went bonkers, shouting questions and holding up cameras and cell phones to snap photos. Mom and Dad shielded me as I was rolled past them into the elevator.

On Chris's floor, the doctors and nurses who were crowded around the door to his room parted to allow us through.

And there he was.

My brother was still hooked up to all the wires and beeping machines I remembered seeing in the ten-second video on Dad's cell phone. He hadn't been shaved in nearly a week, so his beard was now scruffier than I'd ever seen it, and with his tousled hair drooping over his closed eyes, he looked more like a rock star than a football hero. A feeding tube connected him to an IV bag, but even so, I could tell Chris had lost weight.

On the one hand, I was so thrilled to see him that I had to fight the urge to yell, "Hey, Chris!" At the same time, I was shocked to see my big brother looking so pale and . . . *small.*

I caught my breath when a terrifying question popped into my head.

What if he never wakes up?

I bit my tongue so I wouldn't slip and ask it out loud. A lump the size of a baseball formed in my throat. I finally understood how frightened and worried my parents must have been all week.

My bed was wheeled to a spot against the window. Dozens of flower arrangements and balloon bouquets covered every available surface, but they were beginning to droop, as if they were losing hope. Hundreds of unopened cards and letters were piled up on Chris's bedside table. Nurses' shoes squeaked softly on the tile floor, while Chris's monitors beeped faintly. Everybody whispered here, so when the bedside phone rang, we all jumped a little.

"It's for you," Mom said, handing me the receiver. "It's JJ."

"Hey, JJ," I said dreamily into the mouthpiece.

"Omigosh, you're so famous!" JJ screamed. In the background I could hear Cecil making drum and trumpet noises like a one-man band.

"How are you?" JJ asked, but before I could respond, she barreled ahead. "What am I saying? I *know* how you are! It's all over the news! You've got multiple fractures of the right ankle, two broken ribs and a mild concussion."

The concussion was news to me.

"Anyway," JJ went on, "we just wanted you to know that we're handling the press. The stories of Captain Nobody's bravery are filling the airwaves . . ."

". . . and don't forget about the newspapers!" I heard Cecil shout.

"Oh, right . . . we're everywhere."

"Wow" was all I could say. There was a rustling sound on the other end, and the next thing I heard was Cecil's voice: "Hey, man! When can we come see you?"

"I . . . I don't know," I mumbled. "But I'm getting real sleepy, so can I call you guys later?"

"Solid," Cecil said, "but be sure you ask your nurses for tomorrow morning's papers, because I gave those reporters a lot of good quotes."

"And look for our pictures!" JJ chimed in from the background. "They took a ton of pictures."

Mom hung up the phone for me. Dad arrived, carrying a tray of food.

"You hungry, Newt? They've got meat loaf and potatoes and Jell-O."

I was actually starving, but, as drowsy as I was, I couldn't imagine being able to lift a fork.

"Later," I slurred. "But, wait . . . Is Chris any better?"

Mom looked to Dad, who simply said, "Let's talk about that when you've had a little rest."

Before I could object, my eyelids dropped like stones, and I slept.

● ● ●

The growling of my stomach woke me up. I didn't know what time it was, but, except for a faint glow from Chris's machines, the room was dark. I had no idea where Mom and Dad were, but my food tray was gone. My ribs ached and my foot throbbed. I thought about calling a nurse to get another pain shot or something to eat, but I didn't want to cause a fuss.

Because, to tell the truth, I was feeling pretty dumb.

All week I had made such a big deal about getting to the hospital. The whole time I had imagined that if I could just show up at Chris's bedside, I could somehow make a difference. I could tell him about Captain Nobody and the robbery and the plane on the highway. I could tell him silly things, too—like how JJ and

Cecil cut up his old clothes to make my costume, or how I came up with the name Captain Nobody by using the initials C.N. on his T-shirt sleeve.

He would have loved all of that.

But here I was, three feet away from him, and what was I doing? Staring at the ceiling, counting the beeps from his machines. And starving. After all my adventures of the last few days—after all the people I had managed to help in so many ways—I still wasn't able to help my brother.

"Useless," I whispered.

The more that word bounced around in my brain, the more frustrated I got, until I wasn't just upset—I was steamed! And the last time I could remember being that *steamed* was the morning of the Big Game, when I'd whipped up that big, healthy breakfast, and my brother had snored right through it. The last time I'd shouted at him, "Hit the showers!"

Yeah, that's right.

"HIT THE SHOWERS!"

Oh, my gosh. Did I just yell?

Did I really shout in my brother's hospital room?

Oops.

I could still hear my voice echoing off the walls when a pair of nurses burst through the door and raced to my bedside.

"What's wrong?" the first one whispered.

"I'm sorry," I whispered back. "I didn't mean to be loud. I'm never loud, I swear."

"You're in a hospital!" hissed the second.

"I know, I know. Maybe it's because I'm hungry," I tried to explain, "or because my foot hurts, but I promise I won't ever do it—"

Whump!

A pillow hit my head.

The nurses and I exchanged confused looks. *Where did that come from?*

And then, from the bed next to mine, came a hoarse groan.

"I'm up. I'm up."

23

IN WHICH
I WAKE UP
IN THE NEWS

Imagine Christmas morning, New Year's Eve and the Big Game touchdown all happening at the same, exact moment. Our room was suddenly swarming with doctors and nurses and more doctors, all chattering loudly. Mom and Dad pushed their way through the crowd. They hugged and kissed Chris and hugged and kissed me and then hugged Chris again. Doctors shook my hand and ruffled my hair, and the nurses kept hugging us both. And everybody was crying and laughing.

Above the other noise, I heard Chris, in a raspy voice, ask, "How long have I been out?" while doctors kept asking him questions like, "How many fingers am I holding up?" and saying things like, "Amazing!" and, "His vital signs are excellent!"

I tried to raise myself up to get a glimpse of my

brother, but my ribs screamed out, so I flopped back against the pillows. Once I was able to get Mom's attention, though, I said, "Not right now, but when you have a chance . . . can I get a hamburger? And maybe some aspirin?"

"Of course!" She clapped her hands and shouted above the noise in the room, "Everybody!"

They all quieted and turned to her. "Newt is hungry!" she announced. "Can we get him a hamburger, please? Lettuce, no tomato. Lots of mustard. And he's hurting, so, please, give my son—my *other* son—his shot."

Everybody laughed and scattered in many directions. Five minutes later, an official-looking, bleary-eyed woman in a rumpled suit raced in and announced, "The press wants a statement!"

Dad and about six doctors followed her out of the room. As the mob at my brother's bedside thinned, I caught sight of him through the few bodies that still lingered. I wanted to say, "Hey, Chris!" but I figured I shouldn't interrupt all the important medical stuff that was going on. So I lay quietly until a nurse came with my hamburger and another one arrived to administer my pain shot.

Right about then, from the parking lot outside, a loud, long cheer rose up. "Must be the press conference," one of the nurses commented. "Sounds like they just told them the good news."

In the five minutes that it took for me to eat, the

pain medication began to work its magic. I didn't really want to sleep any more, but apparently I wasn't going to have a choice in the matter. As my head began to droop, I turned my face in Chris's direction, hoping I'd catch a peek before I dropped off.

Chris was looking back at me. After being asleep for a week, he still seemed a little dazed, but he smiled and extended an open palm across the space between us. I stretched out my hand to high-five his, and I was *thiiiiis* close to connecting when the tubes and wires in my arm pulled taut. I opened my mouth to speak, to say, "How're you doin'?" but my tongue wouldn't cooperate. Then an orderly with a thermometer stepped between us. In the next instant, I dropped into a deep sleep.

● ● ●

When I finally opened my eyes, the morning sun was streaming in. I looked down the length of the bed, past the enormous white mound of my foot's plaster cast, and was amazed to see my own desk and my own closet.

"Welcome home," came JJ's voice from my bedside. "Sleep enough?"

I turned to find her and Cecil munching on a couple of waffles and shuffling through stacks of newspapers.

"What happened?" I asked in a froggy voice. "How'd I get here?"

"Well, there were so many people crammed around the hospital," JJ explained, "that the police decided to take you out the back way in an ambulance."

"I came home in an ambulance?"

"We all did!" Cecil hooted.

"Your dad invited us to ride along," said JJ, "so we raced down there first thing this morning."

"It was so cool!" Cecil gushed. "There were all these motorcycle cops stopping traffic, so we went *screaming* through every red light!"

"They used the siren?"

"You didn't hear the siren?" he asked. "Man, you *were* out!"

"And check this out," JJ said, holding up a fistful of morning papers. "While you were asleep, we all became stars!"

Every front page carried aerial photographs of me and Reggie Ratner on the roof of the water tower. There were pictures of me falling into the blue inflatable rescue mattress and shots of JJ and Cecil waving at the camera. Thick black headlines screamed: "He Went Up a Nobody, but He Came Down a Hero!" and "Reggie Ratner Rescued by Human Fly."

"And here's a direct quote from me," JJ proudly announced: "'Captain Nobody is now a somebody!'"

They told me about appearing on TV, and how they

had been interviewed by twenty reporters at one time. Cecil even got to perform his drum sounds on a radio show and to demonstrate the Cecil Seesaw on the evening news.

"I decided I'm a natural in front of the camera," he announced.

"But, omigosh, those mobs of photographers . . . the paparazzi?" JJ sighed. "Honestly, Newt, they can be such a pain."

"What about Chris?" I asked. "Did he come home in the ambulance, too?"

"Chris?" laughed JJ. "He left the hospital in a limousine."

"To go where?"

"Where do you think?" Cecil asked as he switched on my small desk TV. *Good Morning, Appleton!* was just starting, and there was Chris being interviewed. He had shaved and showered, and, even though he was a little thinner than usual, he still looked awesome.

"So, Chris Newman," the hostess of *Good Morning, Appleton!* was saying, "after six days in a coma, how are you feeling?"

"Well, my legs are a little wobbly," Chris said in his new raspy voice, "and I'm so hungry that I could eat for a week. But I'm really happy to be back."

He and the hostess laughed. "I think all of Appleton feels the same way," she said. Chris bobbed his head and quietly said, "Thank you."

"And what's this I hear?" said the hostess. "You have a younger brother? Is that true?"

"Yes, it's true, you ninny!" Cecil barked back at the screen.

"Oh, yeah, I have a great brother," Chris smiled on-screen. "Newton. We call him Newt."

"Also known as 'Captain Nobody,'" JJ reminded the TV.

"Newt has become quite the hero, it seems," the hostess continued, holding up the same newspapers that JJ and Cecil had shown me.

"It sure looks that way," Chris answered.

How weird, I thought. I'd spent so much time watching my brother talk about himself on TV, and now there he was, talking about me.

"Now, just before coming on the air with us, Chris, I'm told that you met with the mayor?" the hostess asked.

"I sure did." Chris nodded. "He asked me if I was ready to ride in this year's victory parade."

"And what did you tell the mayor?" the hostess asked.

Chris paused before he answered. "I told him no."

"What?" Cecil, JJ and I all shouted at the screen.

"What?" I could hear my parents yell from downstairs.

"What?" gasped the startled hostess on TV.

"I told the mayor that parades should be led by

heroes," Chris continued, "and I told him that there's only one real hero in Appleton today."

Then he looked directly into the camera so that it felt like he was right there, inside my television set, looking out at me.

"So, what do you say, Newt? Can I ride in your parade?"

• • •

The rest of the afternoon was a blur of phones ringing, doorbells gonging and cars honking as they drove past our house. JJ and Cecil eventually left because now that they were going to be riding in the Appleton parade (that was my only request), they had more interviews to do.

I had some dinner, but because I didn't want to fall asleep and miss seeing Chris again, I refused any more pain medication.

"I'm feeling much, much better," I lied to Dad.

Hours slipped by, and the room grew dark. I tried to watch TV, but every channel kept showing the footage of me falling into the inflatable blue cushion with Reggie dropping on top of me. Finally I switched off the set just as someone behind me cleared his throat.

I turned my head. Chris was standing at my bedside.

"Hey, Captain," he said and smiled.

"Chris," I exhaled sleepily. "Are you home for good?"

"Thanks to you."

He extended his palm.

I slapped him five.

And at that moment, all the hurting stopped.

24

IN WHICH
A LITTLE OLD LADY
MAKES ME LAUGH

The parade took place two days later on a crisp, sunny November Sunday. Because it wasn't just a victory celebration for the Ferrets anymore, the Fillmore High School marching band was joined by Merrimac's band, and together, they made an awesome sound as they strutted through the heart of town.

I was propped up on a dozen pillows in the back of an open convertible. On a little cushion in my lap sat Ferocious the Ferret, tilting his head in constant surprise as throngs of people lining the streets cheered and tossed confetti.

JJ and Cecil rode along with Ferocious and me. Because my ribs were still tender, they did most of the waving.

Right behind us, another convertible carried Chris

and some of his teammates, including Darryl Peeps. Nobody blamed Darryl for knocking out my brother, nor did they continue to blame Reggie Ratner. "It's all a part of the game," my brother said in an interview for the *Appleton Sentinel*, and after that, it seemed like everybody shrugged and forgave everybody else.

I had started using crutches to get around (JJ warned me that if I kept it up, I'd be in danger of developing biceps). When we got to City Hall and I hobbled out onto the stage that had been built over the front steps, the crowd roared and Cecil did an air-drum solo. Then the speeches and presentations began.

First, Fillmore High School got their championship trophy, and the Ferrets all pushed my brother up front to accept the big, gold statue. Next, Mr. and Mrs. Sullivan gave JJ a pair of diamond solitaire earrings to show their appreciation for her part in stopping the robbery.

"From now on, m'dear," Mr. Sullivan announced to JJ, "you are always welcome to correct any sign in our window."

The pilot and the passengers of the plane that made the emergency landing all decided that, if Cecil hadn't volunteered me to take Ferocious home for the night, none of us would ever have been on the highway that day. So they chipped in to buy Cecil a set of drums and a year of lessons.

Plus, they gave Cecil's mom and dad each a pair of earplugs.

Finally, Mr. Clay the locksmith cut a special gold key that he hung on a purple ribbon and laid in a velvet box. As the mayor handed it to me, he declared, "The citizens of Appleton are proud to present the Key to the City to Newton Newman, who has saved many lives and enriched many more."

The crowd clapped and whistled and started whooping, "Newt! Newt! Newt! Newt!"

Looking out over the sea of smiling faces, I saw neighbors and friends of my parents, classmates of mine and teammates of Chris. I spotted Mr. Toomey and Mrs. Young and Mr. Brockman and the nurses and doctors from the hospital. Reggie Ratner was there with his cousin Ricky and the rest of the Merrimac football team. And there were hundreds and hundreds of people I'd never even met, all chanting, "Newt! Newt! Newt!"

How amazing is this? I thought. *They know my name.*

Afterward, on the grounds of City Hall, the bands kept playing as everyone danced and ate and celebrated through the afternoon and into the autumn evening. I hobbled on my crutches from crowd to crowd, meeting new people, shaking hands and posing for pictures. By the time the sun was setting, I was pretty sore and very tired.

"Why don't we get you home?" Dad finally said.

JJ hugged me good-bye and pushed the hair back over her ears to model her diamond earrings. "Imagine, Newt," she whispered as her eyes teared up. "Diamonds like Splendida would wear."

Cecil gave me one of his complicated handshakes. "Do you believe it, man?" he asked. "I'm gonna be a drummer!"

"You always have been," I told him.

When we got home, my parents returned to doing all the things that they would ordinarily do on a November evening. Dad switched his phone back on, and it immediately started ringing, while his beeper vibrated itself right off the kitchen counter.

"Newt, honey," Mom asked, "have you seen the mortgage papers for that house on Hummingbird Lane?"

"Look between the Frosted Flakes and the Cheerios," I answered.

"Of course, of course," she said (as if that made all the sense in the world to file "contracts" with "cereal"), and she headed for the pantry.

In the silence that followed, Chris turned to me and smiled.

"Tired?" he asked.

"Down to the bone."

He took my crutches and put a hand under my arm to help me thump-thump-thump up the stairs to my room. As I got ready for bed, he busied himself by flipping through my sketchbook of mutant crimefighters.

"Wow, Newt. I had no idea," he finally said, looking up. "You're good."

"Thanks," I said quietly. Nothing that had happened that day—not the cheering crowds or the key to the city or even the mayor's speech—nothing made me feel as good as those words.

"So how does it feel to be a hero?" Chris asked as I swung my cast up into bed and eased back onto my pillows.

"I'm not really a hero," I shrugged. "I'm just a kid who happened to be in the right place at the right time, that's all."

He chuckled. "Add a ball to that equation, and you've just described my sports career."

"But you're a . . ." I tried to find the right word, ". . . a *legend*."

"A legend?" He doubled over with laughter as he sat down on the edge of my bed.

"I have to tell you one story," he said, still chuckling. "Today, at City Hall, when we were shaking all those hands and taking all those photographs, y'know, I met this sweet old couple who had read all about your amazing feats. They had driven in from out of state just to be there. I was introduced to them as Chris Newman, and this little, gray-haired lady looks up at me and says, 'Who?'"

"She did not!" I exclaimed.

"She did," Chris insisted. "And so I said, 'Chris Newman? I'm Newt Newman's older brother.' And this lady looks me in the face and says, 'Hmm. I didn't know Newt Newman *had* an older brother.'"

We both laughed so hard that I had to grab my ribs. "Stop! Stop! It hurts!" I said, which only made us laugh some more.

We talked until Mom and Dad popped in to kiss us both good night. After they left, when the whole house got so quiet that we could hear the first winds of winter outside my window, Chris finally sighed and stood up.

"It was a good day," he said, smiling down at me.

"It was," I nodded.

We high-fived each other, and he headed out. But then he stopped at the door of my bedroom with his hand on the light switch.

"Oh, and by the way, bro," he said with a wink, "there's a monster under your bed."

CLICK!